Hunters Hunted

B.E.N.T.
Biological Enhanced Nascent Talent

By Gustavo Bondoni

Three Ravens Publishing
Chickamauga, GA USA

Contents

Chapter 1

It was hot as hell. As usual.

Vernon Pandor strode across the cracked flatness of the Great Sandy Desert which, at least in this particular stretch on its northwestern end, didn't live up to its name. Low green bushes populated the red dirt.

He crossed a road, his bare feet not feeling the heat that must have been more than sufficient to fry eggs. He looked back to see his footsteps marked on the shiny black asphalt and grinned. Someone would wonder what had happened there, how the imprints had been indelibly formed.

In the distance, the sea roared. Just a couple hundred more meters to go.

The sandy beach, a paradise which would have been packed with tourists anywhere else in the world, was deserted as far as the eye could see, and Vernon strode across the sand—which didn't give way as he walked, but supported him just as well as if he were walking across a soft mattress. Again, he left glistening footprints.

Water lapped at his toes, but he didn't slow, his steady cadence taking him into the breakers, then chest high. When the water reached his neck, he paused and looked up into the air. Somewhere up there, above the atmosphere, a satellite would be focusing on him, directing a strike team to come after him.

They should have acted sooner.

He extended his arm, middle finger raised.

"Hope you enjoy explaining the mess to Mr. Wong," he said, wondering if they had enough resolution to read his lips.

Then he closed his mouth, let the water cover his head, and kept walking north. He didn't need to worry about drowning; he could breathe through his skin.

Water dripped from Vernon's body as he emerged from the sea onto a beach that wasn't deserted, but one in which the beachgoers—fishermen and women washing clothes where a stream met the sea—were well trained to see only those things which specifically applied to them. Factions had warred over this stretch of beach since days immemorial, and the price of being an informant was often death.

He caught one man's eye. The man looked away. Good.

Vernon walked up the beach, through the trees just beyond it and onto the road. Once there, he opened the waterproof fanny pack that was the only thing he wore except for a blue Olympic-style swimsuit and pulled out a Garmin GPS system.

The thing was Stone Age technology, but it was a unit that he'd purchased secondhand in the US. No one who mattered knew he had it . . . which meant that no one could track him through its use.

He hummed to himself as he waited for the system to locate a satellite. Then he grunted when the map appeared.

It wasn't all bad news. At least he was on the right island: Sumbawa Island in Indonesia.

But he still had another ten-mile hike to reach the little hut on the beach he was looking for.

He sighed and started walking again. A couple more hours wouldn't make all that much difference.

The house consisted of a sun-bleached wooden frame covered with a rusting galvanized roof. It was much larger than the majority of the houses on the beach—it had at least three rooms that faced the sea—and it had a porch. A black-haired young woman wearing a yellow sundress which contrasted wonderfully with her light-brown skin sat on a porch swing.

Her dark eyes followed him as he approached the house. They tracked him as he climbed the steps, and they stared into him when he stopped in front of her.

Then she sighed. "Fuck," she said. "I thought I told you not to look for me."

"It's not like you went out of your way to hide, Maia," Vernon replied. "I don't think anyone else in Indonesia has one of these." He pushed the porch swing, causing it to sway back and forth. "Marks you out as someone who's been around the world." The young woman tensed, but stayed where she was.

"I like it," she replied. "You should see how the village children swarm over it." She gazed at him for a moment, then shook her head. "Whatever it is, the answer is no. I'm happy here."

"I need help. I'm falling behind."

"That's because what you're trying to do is impossible."

"For one man, yes."

"For a hundred men. Or a thousand. Entire countries have gone after the Triads. Whole police forces. What did that get them? Nothing except for a handful of dead judges and politicos. And a lot more dead cops."

"I burned their SkyBlue lab in the Australian desert," he said. "That will hurt them."

"I know. I saw it on the news. That was a month ago. They've probably rebuilt it by now. Hell . . . they probably rebuilt it in the same place and sent a Talent in there to protect it in case you or the Australians get any ideas about hitting it again."

"I know. That's why I need you. I'm too slow."

Maia sighed. "You're not too slow. You're deluded. The Triads are going to keep doing what they do, shrugging off your silly attempts to get revenge. You should relax, get a beach house." She looked him up and down. "Work on your tan."

"How can you say that after . . ."

"After what? After they forced me to work for them? After they held my family hostage so I'd do what they wanted? After what they did to little Andrea?" She bent down to pick up a drink from the floor. Beads of condensation covered the tall glass. She took a sip. "I'm trying to forget about that. Time heals all wounds, and I've gotten pretty far along the road to healing mine. You know, this island isn't just about Islam. I mean, the Muslims are peaceful, and they help me out, but there are all sorts of older beliefs. The people who follow the traditional naturist practices are much more in touch with the flows of life. I've been studying with them. It really helps."

He looked at the drink. "Can I have one of those?"

"I thought you didn't need to drink. That you got all the sustenance you need through that wonderful skin of yours."

"I like drinking. I like the taste. I like the buzz I get when my skin doesn't interfere and neutralize the alcohol. Hell, sometimes you just need a drink."

Maia shrugged. "Here, take mine. I wasn't really in the mood to get hammered, anyway."

Vernon took a long gulp, reveling in the burning sense of the alcohol going down his throat, barely feeling the pineapple and sugar that gave the drink its taste.

"Look, I really need your help," Vernon said. He reached for Maia's hand.

She disappeared. One second, she was sitting in the chair, the next, she stood behind it, big eyes staring accusingly.

"I'm sorry," Vernon said. "You can come back. I won't touch you."

"That's all right," she replied. Then she smiled thinly. "I suppose I'm not quite as much in tune with the flows of life as I thought before you arrived. But I'm still not going to help. In fact, I'm not going to continue this conversation until you tell me how you found me."

"I'll tell you that when you tell me how you knew I was coming." He held up the drink. "This is still really cold. You haven't been out here long."

They glared at one another for several seconds before Vernon saw Maia's expression change from one of anger to one of annoyance—a subtle change, but one he felt himself experiencing at the same time as he realized who was behind their shared knowledge.

"Rod," they both said at the same time. He said it with a resigned sigh; she did it while stamping her feet.

"Damn," a new voice said. "And here I thought I was being so subtle."

"Shit," Maia said. She pulled a smartphone out of her pocket. It showed the image of a Winnie-the-Pooh avatar speaking on the screen.

Vernon goggled. "You have a phone?"

"Burner phone. Bought it from a junky. Got a prepaid chip from a store in Bali. Untraceable."

"Rod traced it," Vernon pointed out.

"That's because I'm special," Rod's avatar in the phone said. "I can trace anything, anywhere."

Vernon never knew if Rod was BENT or not. By the sheer weight of the man's achievements, Vernon supposed he must be among the ranks of the Biological Enhanced Nascent Talents, but he might just be an incredibly good baseline hacker. No one had ever seen Rod's physical body, so it was hard to check. Even if he was BENT, what would his bend even be? Some kind of intimate relationship with cybernetics? A mind that worked a billion times faster than any computer? The capacity to project his mind into every conceivable electronic device at once? Vernon couldn't even begin to imagine it.

People with weird bends threw him. Maia was easy enough to understand; she could teleport. Even Vernon's own ability, every square centimeter of his epidermis was a massively advanced chemical factory that could instantly recombine the constituent atoms of anything it touched, was simple enough to understand. Rod was a cipher, and that's the way he liked it.

He was also an interfering little git.

"Why?" Vernon asked. "Why lead me back to her when she doesn't want me to be here? And why bother to make it look like an accidental discovery?"

"And why did you show me the feed from that camera so I could wait for him? I thought I'd hit the wrong command by mistake."

Rod grunted. "Because I didn't want you to run when he showed up. It took me nearly two hours to track you down after the last time you disappeared. Do you know how much money I could have made in two hours? I could have bought my own space station."

"That doesn't tell us why you did this. I thought I'd been lucky with my searches," Vernon said.

"You're a Neanderthal, and Maia isn't stupid," Rod said. "You would never have found her. Hell, the Triads will never find her, and trust me, they're looking." The Winnie-the-Pooh leered at them. "Every once in a while, I send them a false trail or two. They're combing the Peruvian mountains for you as we speak."

"Thanks," Maia said.

"I've got your back."

"You always did. Except that you sent this one after me," Maia said. "And I really want to know why. No cute attempts to distract me. Just tell me why."

"It's time." Rod said.

"Time for what?" Vernon replied.

"Time to stop screwing around with your stupid little revenge against the Triads. They don't matter."

"Tell that to the millions of people whose lives they fuck up every year. Or to the hundreds of thousands they own outright," Vernon snapped.

"No need to tell them. They already know. Because in almost every single case, they went to the Triads first. For a loan, for a woman, for a fix, for a game of chance. Sure there are exceptions— especially in the white slavery trade—but they're exceptions," Rod said. "And I'm talking about something big." The Pooh icon turned to stare at Maia. "And you need to leave off the whole spirituality thing. You're not getting anywhere, and you never will. You can't forget what happened to your family, because that's not the way you're wired. Time won't heal you . . . but maybe having a purpose will."

"And what noble purpose are you proposing?"

"I propose," Rod replied, "that we avoid the death of every single person on the planet with a bend. Everyone from some little kid who can change the color of his pee to Emperor Hijiro himself. If we don't act right away, they're going to kill every last BENT on the planet."

Chapter 2

"**Y**ou're bullshitting us. It's been tried before. No one can kill all the BENT. Hell, that's even if you can find them in the first place," Vernon said.

"I'm dead serious," Rod said.

"How?" Maia asked. "There are BENT out there whose power is to digest everything perfectly. They don't know it. Some can make their hearts transparent. They don't know it either. Does anyone think they can find people who don't even know they're BENT?"

"I . . ." The Pooh shrugged. "All I know is that they've developed a weapon that works with gene markers . . ."

"Again, bullshit. There aren't any definitive markers," Vernon said.

"Combined with radiation signals. Possibly neutrino signatures," Rod replied. He let that sink in. "Look, they haven't exactly gone out of their way to publish the results in *Nature*. But they're out there, and they're about to begin large-scale testing."

"Why should we believe that?" Maia asked.

"Have I ever lied to you?"

"I don't know. Have you?"

"No."

"Then broadcast this to the world," Vernon said. "Tell the Emperor. And if he doesn't do anything about it, call in Alex Lloyd. He likes to kill people and break things wholesale. We're just bit players."

"If you guys won't believe me, what makes you think they will?"

"Self-preservation? They'll check it out just on general principles. Tell them where to hit, and there will be a smoking crater at whatever site you pick out," Vernon said.

"That's the problem. Before we can do that, we need to find out exactly where the facility is located. And if we tip anyone else off, they'll hear of it and hide even deeper." He paused and looked around significantly. "And they're so deeply hidden that even I'm only getting the barest hints and the slightest whiff of smoke. But I've smelled enough to be convinced there's fire."

"And you're the best, so if you haven't found them, no one else will, right?" Maia asked.

"Yeah. I am the best. On par with a couple of computer-focused Talents, but probably even better than they are. And I know what I know."

Vernon drained the drink, enjoying the sense of alcohol burning a path down his throat. He should drink more, he thought. "So, who are these evildoers who want to kill 15 percent of humanity?"

"I'll give you three guesses," Rod replied.

"I don't need three guesses," Maia said. "I can get it in one. It's one of those Human Rights groups, right? One of the ones that says baseline humans are getting a bad deal because the BENT are taking all the power and money."

"As if they'd ever let us have power and money if we didn't take it," Vernon said.

"Of course not," Maia said. "Because they're scared of us."

"All right," Rod said with an exaggerated sigh from his Pooh avatar. "So, full marks for knowing what drove the project, but you get a zero for your attempts to guess who it was. I mean, I can't very well credit you guys for guessing that baseline humans are behind this . . . the BENT aren't going to create a secret project to kill themselves. But you still haven't guessed who is behind it."

"Not the rights groups?" Vernon asked.

"No. They'd be much too obvious. In fact, they probably exist to make a lot of noise and draw attention away from the real culprits."

Maia and Vernon exchanged a glance. "We give up," she said.

"It's the Norwegian Faction," Rod said.

"What in the world is the Norwegian Faction?" Maia asked.

"They're terrorists," Rod replied. "The dark web, even the part open to any noob with the NewTor browser installed, is alive with them."

"We don't use the dark web, Rod," Vernon said. "Not even as noobs."

"Jeez. You guys are no fun." He paused. "But that doesn't matter. What matters is whether you're in or not."

"No," Maia said. "Not like this. Not just because you say so."

"I need more proof," Vernon replied.

"Oh. You'll have it. Both of you will. But you need to wait for a week or so. Besides, I'm putting together the rest of the team."

"Get heavy hitters," Vernon said.

"I'll get who I can without spooking the quarry," Rod said.

Maia's phone went dark.

"Dammit," Vernon said. "I can't believe he's pulling this crap again." He inspected his glass. "And this seems to have emptied itself."

"Come inside," Maia said with a sigh. "I'm going to need one, too."

"Why's that?"

"Because I assume the next conversation we're going to have is about you staying here for the next week, or however long it takes Rod to do his cat herding."

Vernon chuckled. "The idea had occurred to me."

"Fuck," she said. Then she held up a hand. "If you say that that idea had occurred to you, too, I'll teleport myself so my hand is around your heart. Then I'll squeeze until your eyes pop out of your head. Let's see if your magic skin can protect you from that."

"Jeez," Vernon said. "You sleep with a girl once, and she immediately thinks that's all you want her for."

"So, you weren't thinking about trying your luck?" she asked.

"I can't answer that question, because I don't think I'd enjoy having my heart squeezed," Vernon replied.

"You know," Maia said as she nestled against his chest, "I wasn't planning on this. I'd been fine over the past year, just being by myself."

Vernon grinned. "And I was fine sleeping on the cot in the other room. You had no obligation to come and get me."

"I missed you."

He leaned over and kissed her hair. "And I missed you. But do you really think anything's changed? We're still the same trainwreck we were before. The one thing that unites us—the only thing we really have in common—is the rage we have for the people we've lost. For the way we lost those people. Is that enough to keep us together?"

"Who said anything about staying together? The way I see it is Rod will probably either produce proof or fake it well enough that we'll join his suicide mission, and we'll both end up dead before it's over. And even if we say no, our life expectancy is measured in months. The Triads are going to catch up with you sooner or later with some weapon you can't just neutralize. And I have to see the attack coming if I want to be able to jump away from it. A sniper on a hill can blow me away an hour after they figure out where I am. And if Rod could do it, so can they, no matter what he says."

"So, jump away now," Vernon replied. "Jump to the middle of the Amazon. Jump to Patagonia. Let them follow a cold trail."

Maia sighed. "Look out that window."

"I know what's out there," he replied.

"Humor me. Look out the window. What do you see?"

He disentangled himself and crossed to the open window. "I see the sea under the moonlight. The waves breaking against the beach."

"And what do you feel?"

"I feel the soft, warm breeze against my chest, and I smell the salt in the air. Okay. I get it. This is paradise, and you don't want to leave."

"It's not just that," Maia said. He heard the rustle of the sheets, saw her form—a darker shadow in the dark—sitting straight on the bed. "It's that I want to live a normal life. I don't want to spend the rest of my existence staying one step ahead of some gang of goons."

"So, you've decided to opt for quality of life over quantity? I guess I can understand that."

"Why does it have to be short? I came here because by being here I pose no threat to anyone. It's supposed to be a message in and of itself. I'm out of the game, and I'm prepared to let bygones be bygones. Why can't the world accept that?"

"First, you know too much, and you've done too much damage to be allowed to just fade away. And second, the fact that you're here means absolutely nothing. I can be counted on to stay in one place. You can't. All you have to do is blink, and you can be anywhere you want."

"I want to be here. And right now, I'm happy to be here with you. This is all I ask. Is that so much?"

He climbed back into the bed, and she put her head back on his chest. "It's not too much to ask. But some people won't even give you that unless you twist their arms."

Three hours later, the TV turned itself on at full volume.

Vernon jumped out of the bed and fumbled for a weapon. A knife, a gun, a shoe . . . anything in reach.

He realized that it wasn't just the TV. Maia's laptop, her cell phone, and even the GPS he'd tossed on the table and left there were all on. All of them had Winnie-the-Pooh staring out from them.

"Run," the myriad Poohs yelled. "Now."

A hand gripped Vernon's forearm . . .

. . . and suddenly, he wasn't standing on the dry wood of the bedroom floor, but on the sand of the beach inside a clump of trees.

"Is that your house?" he whispered to Maia, who'd appeared beside him.

"Yes," she hissed back. "Now shut up. I want to see what's going on."

The sea splashed, and a black Zodiac tactical boat appeared on the beach. A single person descended from it, visible only because of the contrast between his black clothes and the white sand of the beach, illuminated by stars and the distant glow of streetlights.

The figure knelt on the beach and began to assemble what looked like a missile launcher. In a well-practiced ritual, the weapon was quickly built and placed on one shoulder.

A trail of flame illuminated the night, a line that ended at the open window.

A moment later, the house exploded into splinters. No flames, no huge fireball; one minute, the structure stood there, window open to the sea, the next, tiny bits of it were falling on the beach.

"That asshole," Maia said.

Vernon put his hand on her arm. "You do know that the guy might have done you the greatest favor ever, don't you? If he filmed what just happened, it might get the Triads off your back. Hell, if they knew I was in there, too, they might leave me alone long enough to . . . ."

"To what? To knock over another of their facilities, which will immediately make them realize you're still alive, and therefore, so am I?"

"You're right. This might be an opportunity for both of us to start over."

The figure in black stepped back into the Zodiac and, with a muted rumble, disappeared into the waves.

"Want to go see what's left?" Vernon asked.

He could barely see Maia shaking her head in the dark. "No," she said. "There was nothing in there I can't live without. Are you coming?"

"Coming where?"

"With me." She put her hand on his arm.

"I guess," he replied. "Where are you thinking of—"

The world around them blinked away.

Chapter 3

Juan Estevez drifted on the wind, just coherent enough to stay in one piece as the wind pushed him over the mountains. He was at peace with the world, watching the Los Angeles Basin appear in the distance.

Suburban sprawl, barrios mixed with mansions, industrial parks, and low-rent neighborhoods all tied together by expressways that separated each class of citizen from the rest, while at the same time allowing them to mix together.

He cohered a little more, and gravity tugged at his body, taking him into a crosswind that blew him north.

The barrio in which he'd been born and raised drifted beneath him, and he allowed gravity's tug to get a little stronger, a little stronger until he landed on the sidewalk at a comfortable walking pace, his body completely solid.

No one paid him any heed. Anyone who noticed him would probably have thought he was just another of those BENT who could do a little limited flying, nothing to write home about.

That was fine. He didn't need the hassle right now. Besides, just landing and walking to his safe house meant he could choose his landing spot. The government couldn't watch every corner in LA, could they?

The house was a small, run-down place built on a tiny plot that looked exactly like every one of its neighbors. The blinds were down, and the place had the look of gentle neglect you'd expect from an unoccupied home in a suburb. The only concession he'd made to being a good neighbor was to hire a gardener to keep his tiny patch of lawn trimmed to civilized levels.

He glanced around. No one was paying him the least bit of attention, so he allowed himself to drift into a thin cloud—thinner than anything science could imagine as being a single entity—and drifted through the door. Paint, primer, wood, primer, paint, each layer completely distinct to him as he passed through them.

Finally, he stood in the living room of the house he'd bought under a different name and had furnished by a childhood friend, a contractor who thought the house was for Juan's aunt.

He smiled. The guy had gone completely overboard with the pinks and florals, but the work was high-quality, and the man had probably charged Juan's apocryphal aunt much less than he would have charged a gringo.

Not that it mattered. When you could walk through walls, getting money was not exactly hard. He dropped onto a flower-covered easy chair and sighed. It had been a long day. Profitable, but long.

"Hello, Mr. Estevez," a man's voice said. "I was beginning to think you'd never use this place."

The man was completely bald, and his blond eyebrows were barely visible, giving Juan the impression that he was talking to an egg with eyes. He didn't jump, didn't even feel any fear. Instead, he mostly felt annoyance that his preparations had been so completely useless. Also curiosity as to who had penetrated his defenses and why.

After all, if the guy pulled out a gun or did anything else suspicious, Juan would turn into a cloud of subatomic particles.

It was hard to hurt a cloud of subatomic particles unless you were BENT in a very specific way. It wasn't the kind of talent the government went out of its way to look for.

"And who the fuck are you?" Juan asked.

"My name isn't important, but you can call me Lars if you must have a label." The man spoke

English with an accent, but this was LA. Half the people here spoke with an accent. And the other half didn't speak the language at all.

Besides, this guy's accent didn't sound Latino or African. This guy was *fancy*. Eurotrash gangster, then.

"That seems fair, since you know who I am. So, Lars, who do you want me to spy on? What impenetrable security system needs penetrating? What do you need stolen?" He raised his hands. "And please don't waste your time trying to justify yourself to me. I don't care why you need me to do what you want me to do. I just care how you can pay me. And remember, I can get all the money I want, so you'll have to put up something more interesting than cash."

"You've got me all wrong," the man said with a sad smile.

"That's what they all say."

"Yes . . . but in my case, it's true. You see, I'm not a client."

"Oh," Juan said, tensing in case it was time to make a fast exit. He studied the man again, but unless the guy was BENT in some unusual way, he didn't look threatening. Just a bald guy in a white button-down shirt and ridiculously unfashionable chinos holding a cell phone. Hell, he looked like an office worker from central casting in a European drama film. "Then what are you?"

"I'm an executioner," the man said. He looked down at his phone and fiddled with something, swiping this way and that.

Juan laughed, but just in case, he began to decohere a little.

Nothing happened.

"What?"

"Oh. That," Lars said, looking up from his phone. "I have control of your bend. Just give me a second while I work this."

"What the fuck is happening?" Juan shouted. He tried to stand, but his leg went into the floor and the rest of him stayed where it was. He looked down to look at his leg . . . and looked *through* his leg instead. Only his leg was gaseous, almost invisible. That couldn't be. That wasn't how it worked. His whole body changed, or nothing did.

He tried to grab the man, but his arms, far from being gaseous, had gone completely in the other direction. They were completely stiff, locked solid. It was a trick he'd used often, because in this state, he was impervious to any form of penetration. So, bullets—or cars or trains—would simply bounce off him without damaging him in the least.

"What are you doing to me?"

Lars fiddled with the phone a bit more. "Just testing out some new stuff we've been working on. This phone is connected to a machine over there— yes, I know you can't turn to look, and I'm not going to release you right now, so you'll have to trust me on that. Anyway, the machine is connected to your bend on a cellular level. It's manipulating your power for its own use."

"That's impossible," Juan said.

Lars shrugged. "Judge for yourself."

He fiddled with the phone a little more, and Juan felt himself growing diffuse.

Good, he thought when he went past the threshold he knew meant that any physical attack would just sail right through him. *At least he can't hurt me now.*

He knew that if the man calling himself Lars was telling the truth about being able to manipulate his bend—and it sure looked that way—the state of grace wouldn't last. The man could bring him back to baseline level, pull out a handgun—or a kitchen knife—and kill him. Of course, if he brought him to regular density, Juan would fight like the third monkey on the ramp to Noah's Ark. So, they had a stalemate.

What? Wait!

The diffuse cloud of disparate atoms that was Juan stretched. Then he stretched some more, further than he normally did. Then, that sadist, Lars, hit a command and pulled him even thinner.

Thin enough that it began to hurt. Juan could actually feel the tenuous bonds between his components tear.

He screamed, and it was the sound of the wind whispering through the trees. Or maybe even more tenuous than that.

Though the sound might have been imperceptible, the agony was almost overwhelming. He screamed, he cursed, he begged for the oblivion of death, or at least unconsciousness. But none of that came.

Juan felt each and every bond snap as his subatomic parts drifted into a gas too tenuous to exist.

Then he scattered to the winds, gone for good.

The man calling himself Lars stopped the car in front of a suburban house. He checked the address on his list and confirmed that the GPS system hadn't brought him to the wrong Peach Drive.

The house was a perfectly ordinary upper-middle-class dwelling. It sat on a patch of grass green enough to satisfy the local HOA, and Lars could see a large backyard and a wooden deck behind the house. The siding was brick, and the design colonial, but if you studied the contemporary-style house next door, you would probably find that the houses were almost identical in overall shape—the only differences being the siding itself and a few trim details.

He took a deep breath before approaching the front door. Though he'd eliminated Estevez, a dangerous man and a Talent, he actually considered this assignment to be more difficult. His superiors and the technical team would have disagreed with him and attempted to force him to build up to his confrontation with Estevez, which meant that they would have asked him to come here before going to the barrio.

He smiled. That was the nice thing about being in deep cover: the nannies back at HQ couldn't contact him often enough to break his balls and change his plans.

Lars opened the trunk and pulled out a briefcase. The equipment inside was heavy, but it wasn't fragile, which meant that he would only need to carry it to the door, and then he could lay it on the ground.

He did so now, careful not to let it tip over and fall on one of his feet—that would hurt—and made sure his collar was straight. The next bit would be a lot easier if he made a decent impression.

The walk up to the door consisted of flat stones cutely and artistically set in the grass, and the doorbell actually played the movie-staple ding-dong chime. Thin windows as tall as the entrance flanked the dark wooden door on both sides. They were covered with white curtains.

Before the door opened, a curtain twitched as the inhabitants of the house inspected him; this might be a good neighborhood, but it was still LA. Lars pretended not to notice and kept his eyes on the door.

Finally, the door opened to reveal a blonde woman in sweatpants and a pink sweater. Her hair was tied in a bun. "Yes?" she asked.

"I'm from the Census Bureau," Lars said, holding up a card. The card was real; the name on it was an actual Census Bureau employee, but the photo was of Lars. If she checked, it would pass muster. Except the real employee was working in San Diego at that particular moment, not in LA. "Could I have ten minutes of your time?"

She hesitated, stared at the card for a moment, then shrugged. "Sure. It's not like I have anything else going on at the moment."

"Thank you, I really appreciate it. It's just a quick questionnaire. You are Mrs. Elaine Coventry of 3345 Peach Drive, correct?"

"Yes, that's me."

"Excellent. How many people live in this household?"

"Four. Me, my husband, and two little girls. They're at school now."

He pretended to input the data into the tablet he was carrying. What he was really doing was to power up the machine inside the briefcase.

"Ah. How old are they?"

"Six and eight."

"And how many bedrooms do you have in the house?"

"There are three of them, but we only use two: one for us and one for the girls. The other one is my husband's study. Well, I use it to do yoga, too."

"All right," he said. The graph on the tablet was nearly at 100 percent. He had to keep her talking for a few more seconds. "And cars?"

"Two. Keith's Mercedes and my Prius."

"Very good. Do you have any bends in the household? This question isn't obligatory, by the way."

"Oh, it's no secret. I can turn my hair blue."

"No one else?" Lars asked.

"No . . . Keith is baseline, and the girls haven't hit puberty yet. You know they say most bends manifest at puberty."

Lars smiled and hit a command. Elaine's hair began to turn a bright electric blue.

But he wasn't looking at her head, he was staring at the tiny hairs on her arm. They also turned blue, giving her pale skin an unhealthy look.

"Just one moment," he said. "I'm pulling up the follow-up set of questions." He smiled apologetically. "They autogenerate based on your initial answers, but unfortunately, my cell connection isn't as good as it should be."

The tablet told him that the process was proceeding as it should. In her case, her bend wasn't powerful enough to pull her apart. But the process that was harmless in her hair . . .

. . . would be really, really toxic in the rest of her body.

"Excuse me," Elaine said. "I'm not feeling well. I think I need to sit down."

Her face had changed tone, not quite the same shade of her hair, but a deep light-blue color. Her breathing was ragged, and she stumbled in her attempt to sit down.

"Help me," she whispered, barely able to get the words out.

"I could," Lars replied. "But I really need to know if this process works." He looked down at her and smiled. "But you've been very helpful. In fact, I have only one more question: do the carpets match the drapes?"

For a fraction of a second, Elaine Coventry stopped pulling at her clothes in a vain attempt to loosen her shirt and stared at him. She understood the question, had probably been asked the same thing by every guy who tried to pick her up in a bar after she told him about her bend. Habit turned her expression to a quick note of controlled fury that cut through the terror of being unable to breathe. Then, with a choking wheeze, she fell onto her side and remained still.

Lars studied her for a moment, tempted to have a look for himself.

Then he shrugged and turned away. "Not worth it. She's BENT."

He shuddered, closed the door carefully behind him with a cloth in order not to leave any fingerprints, and walked back to his car.

The next address on his list was on Wilshire Ave.

A guy who grew extra fingers on random parts of his body, whether he wanted it to happen or not.

"It might be interesting to see what an extra finger right into his brain would look like," Lars said to himself as he pulled away from the curb.

Chapter 4

Ignoring the knife, Vernon smiled at the guy. He glanced Maia's way. "How do you say 'You really don't want to do that?' in Portuguese?" he asked.

"I don't think he cares," Maia replied. "He looks like the kind of guy who enjoys carving tourists up and then raping their dates."

Vernon looked back at the mugger. The man glared at him, the seething anger palpable behind the dark-brown eyes. The assailant shouted something in Portuguese and waved his knife under Vernon's eyes. He didn't seem to expect them to do anything—it almost appeared that he was just shouting to make the experience worse for them.

"You know," Vernon said, "I think you're right. Still, it's too bad about the suit. I liked this one."

"Then try to get him to stab you in the face or something," Maia replied.

"He'll never go for that. No one who gets his rocks off knifing people will go after the face. That's a good way to lose a fight. Besides, it has to be more satisfying to watch a guy die from a bleeding gut wound, knowing he's dead, but still being alive."

The wide-eyed man stared at them in disbelief, eyes large and white in his light-brown face. He was just another of a million small-time thugs who roamed the back alleys of Brazil's beach towns, looking for tourists who strayed too far from the bright lights of the main drags. The fact that his victims were just standing around talking calmly appeared to infuriate him. With a scream, he dove forward and plunged his knife into Vernon's stomach.

Vernon felt the impact. Felt the man's hand against the cloth of his suit.

But when the attacker pulled the knife away, all he saw was a hilt. A smoking hilt.

"I hope that wasn't too expensive," Vernon said.

The man's eyes widened, but before he could react, Vernon closed the gap between them and put his hands on his cheeks.

Vapor rose from the spot where Vernon's hands contacted the man's skin, and hot tropical air was filled with the scent of melting plastic. Vernon—other than vaguely being able to communicate his intentions—had little control over which chemical reaction his skin would induce. In fact, he had zero knowledge of chemistry or the forces involved except to know that he could only operate with what was already there.

So the knife might have oxidized instantly or simply melted into vapors of iron . . . Or it might have undergone some unknown and exotic operation Vernon would never understand. But he couldn't transform iron into gold.

Vernon watched the man with interest. Whatever reaction his touch had initiated in the mugger's skin had expanded inwards, and now, it appeared the man's entire face was melting. The smell of burning insulation intensified, and the man tried to scream, but all that emerged was a strangled gurgle.

Vernon took a step back and watched the rest of the show. Then he took another step away. Whatever had initiated with the contact, the reaction was self-sustaining and enormously exothermic. It was hot.

He turned to Maia. "Wow, I've never seen this one before. I generally have to hit them a bunch of times and burn them bit by bit. Of course, they're usually hitting me back and burning themselves at the same time, and usually dissolving their hands. But this is a new one."

Maia grimaced. "I bet he was high on something weird, and the chemicals caused it to go like this."

He shrugged. "I wish I could control it."

Vernon took her hand and led her away from where the man was dissolving into a pile of goo and clothing. Two blocks later, they came to the little cabin beside the dirt road where they'd made their home for the past two weeks. It wasn't on the tourist side of town—in fact, it was out of town, alongside a dirt road in the middle of the woods—but it had a view of the beach from the front of the house.

"I don't know," Maia said.

"Don't know what?"

"If you'd be better off controlling it. You wouldn't have time to react." She opened the door and walked through the single room to open the shutters. "For starters, you'd be vulnerable to bullets. You could never react quickly enough to order your skin to protect you from a bullet you never saw. That's my problem: I'm easy pickings for snipers. Unless I can see the attack coming, I can never teleport away in time to survive. You can just sit there, and if the bullet touches your skin . . . poof . . . gone."

"Yeah. You're right. And I know it, too. But sometimes . . . I didn't want to kill that guy, you know."

"He deserved it. We weren't resisting, we weren't trying to run. We were just standing there, and he knifed you. Do you think you'd have been the first? And do you think he'd have left me alive after whatever he did to me once you were out of the way? I think the piece of shit deserved exactly what he got."

"I suppose. Do you think my bend somehow knows those things? Do you think that's why it did that to him?"

"It might," Maia replied. "That's how it knows enough to vaporize a bullet that touches you and to turn everything on my skin into pleasure hormones or something."

Vernon looked up at her. "What? It does that?"

"Oh, yeah. Why do you think I have such a hard time saying no to you? On one hand, I know we're never going to agree on almost anything. On the other . . . let's just say that the way sex feels with you is better than anything I've felt, except one time with a guy whose bend was . . ." She chuckled. "Let's just say it was explicitly sexual, and it had more than one facet. But he would never have stayed with one girl. He was too enamored of the way they swooned over his little party trick to limit himself to one. But you . . . that chemical factory of yours . . ."

She let her dress drop to the floor and stood silhouetted, a dark shadow against the slightly less dark of the light through the window.

"I'm waiting," Maia said.

The mugger's death was the talk of the little seaside village for the following week. It seemed the man had come in from Sao Paulo and had robbed several tourists further south, killing at least five men and, as Maia suspected, abusing several women. The question on everyone's mind was who the hero had been who decided to melt the bastard in acid to the point where the cops had needed to scrape skin from an unaffected part of the guy's body to run a DNA match.

Everyone seemed to agree that this was the correct way to deal with scum in human form.

Vernon and Maia heard the talk, but didn't participate. He wondered what they would have thought if they knew that the same power that had allowed him to destroy the monster whose death they celebrated made Vernon himself live in perpetual fear that someday a four-year-old would run into him with a bicycle and get turned into a pile of ash.

Still, he listened to the men and women—mostly Brazilian holidaymakers from inland cities—talk about the man's death in openly approving terms and smiled along. He'd been adopted as their pet gringo, a guy who could be counted on to drink at their same rate and enjoy the same bawdy stories.

And all was at peace until the day he noticed one of the cars acting funny.

A Ford SUV was parked alongside the road, and he heard a soft whir as he passed. The driver's side mirror moved into place as if the driver were adjusting it to his position.

Except there was no driver in the car. It was empty.

Vernon, who'd been returning to the house to keep a lunch date with Maia after a morning of chatting and playing cards with the men—they played a game called *Truco,* which used Spanish playing cards and which they said had been brought to the little town by hordes of Argentine tourists before that country's most recent economic collapse—redoubled his pace.

"Maia," he said as he entered the house. "We need to get the hell out of here."

She was sitting on one of the soft chairs in the living room—wooden structures with large plastic pillows. She turned to face him. "It's too late, I'm afraid."

A small white drone with a screen—essentially a cell phone with propellers—hung in the air just in front of the window.

Winnie-the-Pooh looked out at them.

"Dammit, Rod," Vernon said. "You just don't give up, do you?"

"I can't, Rod replied. You two are the very best for what needs to be done. You're not plugged into any of the big organizations that could mess everything up, and you've got gifts. Your bends are really special."

Maia glared at the little helicopter. "Rod was just about to tell me how he found us this time."

"You shouldn't have killed that murderer," Rod said. The image of the little bear gave a tiny shrug. "It brought up all kinds of red flags . . ."

Maia stamped her feet. "No way. That guy couldn't have been more than local news. Not even regional. And even here, the news only gave him a couple of days coverage. The only people talking about him are in the bars. I don't buy it."

"Well, I had my trawlers looking for exactly that kind of thing."

"And how did you identify us? There must have been thousands of incidents that fit our profile every day."

Unlike Vernon, who preferred to live his life in blissful ignorance of technical subjects like electronics—and particularly chemistry—Maia liked to know how things worked. She was smart, and if she hadn't fallen into the clutches of the Chinese mafia so early in her life, she would probably have tried to make a life for herself as an engineer. Although, considering how tough it was to survive as just another engineer among the teeming masses of Asia—even before the upheaval caused by Emperor Hijiro—they might, in a cruel and callous way, have done her a favor.

"I hacked into the municipal security cameras. But they only cover a couple of blocks around the town square, so I used vehicle reversing cameras and facial recognition programs."

"In thousands of possible locations?" Maia asked.

"What can I say? I'm just that good," Rod replied. "Look, I know it sounds like an enormous waste of resources, but I had a good reason for tracking you down. They killed my ghost."

"Who killed whom?" Maia said. "And what the hell is a ghost?"

"The people I was telling you about killed a man called Juan Estevez. He was a ghost in the sense that he could go through any security system ever created without being spotted."

Vernon jumped in, "And how do you know these mysterious genocidal BENT-haters of yours were responsible? Did they leave a business card or something? I mean . . . this ghost guy sounds like the kind of dude who would have a ton of enemies."

"His bend was to be able to disperse the molecules of his body to the density he wanted— to a certain degree. The Norwegian Factor has a machine that can kill you by using your own bend against you. In his case, they simply spread him so thin, he broke."

"How can you possibly prove that?" Vernon asked.

"It was caught on Estevez's security cameras . . . and I recorded it before they went in and deleted everything. You want to watch?"

Without waiting for a reply, the image of Pooh disappeared, to be replaced by the interior of a small house. A man sat in a chair.

Actually, a man sat mostly on a chair, except for one leg, which appeared to have been embedded into the chair. As Vernon watched, he seemed to inflate like a balloon, growing ever more transparent as he did so. Even through the distortion of the grotesque blowing-up, the expression of pain and terror on the man's face could be made out quite clearly. Then he simply disappeared, a balloon popped by a pin.

The man in the room with him picked up a briefcase, spat onto the chair, and let himself out.

"Who was that?" Maia asked.

"Just an operative," Rod replied. "The Norwegian Factor has dozens of them. This particular one has slaughtered five of the BENT in Los Angeles. Except for the ghost, they were all perfectly innocent people whose only crime was to be BENT. And, just like Mr. Estevez there—who I wanted to recruit to our mission—he used their own bend against them."

Maia snorted. "That's stupid. Bends don't hurt their owner. Ever. It's one of the few absolute truths in the world. You can't go faster than light, and your own bend won't hurt you."

"And yet, you teleport from place to place faster than light," Rod replied.

"Fuck," Maia said.

"Yeah. Think of bends like cellular division. It's what allows you to grow, what makes your bones knit when you hurt yourself. What keeps your body healthy. But when it becomes uncontrolled . . ."

"Cancer," Maia said.

"Precisely." The little Pooh cartoon gave them a significant look. "Now, if I could find you guys, so can the people we're up against. How'd you like that chemical factory of yours to eat through your skin, Vernon? And Maia, how much fun would you have if you jumped into the center of the sun? Or if half of you went one way and the other half another? Both of those are possible."

"Fuck," Maia said again.

Rod reeled off a set of coordinates, a bunch of numbers that Vernon couldn't follow. Maia nodded. "All right."

She held out her hand, and Vernon sighed and took it.

Their little love nest in Brazil winked out of sight.

They reappeared in a dingy apartment. A cold, dingy apartment where a woman who couldn't have been more than nineteen or twenty jumped when they appeared. She faded into half-invisibility when they showed up, making it look like her clothes hung in the air.

"Wait," the unseen woman said. "You can make your clothes travel with you? That's unfair."

Chapter 5

"Ah," a voice from the TV said. "So nice to get the gang together."

The annoying tones that had grown so familiar came from the TV.

Vernon glared at Rod. "Can't you choose a different avatar?"

"Haven't you heard? Pooh is in the public domain now. I can use him however I want."

"I'm pretty sure that version of Pooh is still covered. As if you ever cared about lawyers," Maia replied. "I suppose you can take down all of Disney's systems in a heartbeat if they decide to come after you."

"They'd have to find me to come after me," Rod replied. "Now, I believe some introductions are in order. Sarena is the team's new ghost. She isn't just invisible to the eye, but to any kind of instrument made to detect electromagnetic waves, including infrared and x-rays. They might know she's there, but they won't see her coming."

"Hi," the now-invisible woman said from somewhere inside the floating clothes.

"Maia is our transportation specialist, and she is special. As you mentioned, unlike other people with a teleport bend, she doesn't need to be starkers to move around—she can bring her clothes. Better still, she can bring the team. With their clothes." Pooh shrugged. "Well, except for Sarena's clothes. Not much use as a forward scout if your underwear is bobbing around in midair, I'm afraid."

"Hi," Maia said. Then she winked at Sarena. "I've known Rod for almost a decade, and you'll be happy to know he doesn't get any better when you get to know him."

"Finally," Rod continued, "this is Vernon. His friends would call him Vern, except he doesn't have any. He's our version of the unmovable object. Nothing can penetrate his skin without getting transformed into something else, and even things like heat can't hurt him, because he can turn the very air around us into an endothermic reaction that sucks heat out of the air."

"Or something like that," Vernon said. "Hi."

"Now that we all know each other, we just need to wait for the final member of our team, our irresistible force. Well, forces. There's two of them, and their bend is that, when they hold hands, they become super strong. Think superman, but unable to fly." The door buzzer rang. "That must be them, now. Perfect timing."

"Yeah," Vernon said. "I imagine you weren't watching the building's security feed to announce them just as they arrived. You'd never do that."

A man and a woman entered the apartment. Their skin was so black as to look almost blue, and they appeared to be in their forties. They were both trim and tall—she appeared to be at least six feet tall, and he was half a head taller. "This is the Prince and Princess," Rod said. "They came specially from Kenya to help us out in this little project."

Vernon's trepidation as he shook the man's hand must have shown, because the prince grinned. "Don't worry, I can't pulverize your fingers unless I'm holding hands with my sister. Otherwise, I'm just a regular guy. Hell, you could probably best me two out of three falls on any given day."

The prince's accent made Vernon feel like he had dung on his shoes and dirt behind his ears. The man could have gone to Oxford, chosen the most traditional English don on the faculty, and made that man sound like a country bumpkin. His tones were cultured, clipped, and superior.

"I'm charmed to meet you," the princess said, holding out her hand for him to shake. He resisted the urge to kiss it, but the woman's tone made her brother sound almost pedestrian.

She smiled, showing perfect, dazzling teeth. "I can't break you either. Not right now, anyway."

"I'm happy to hear it," he replied. To himself, however, he was thinking, *You can break my heart, though.* "So, what are you prince and princess of?"

Her smile faltered. "Our kingdom, sadly, no longer exists. Tribal realignment and the whole movement to expel the colonists from Africa—with the nation-state-building that accompanied that—put our traditional land in a place where no less than four borders come together. And our people were subsumed. Some were massacred. Unfortunately, we weren't alive at the time to defend them . . . and the BENTs our people did have were weaker than those of our neighbors. Those were dark times."

"So, they're currently living as royalty in exile with nothing to their names but a few billion dollars, a couple of mansions, a fleet of yachts, and the protection of the British crown. A terrible fate."

"Don't make me come over there, you little computer freak," the prince said. But he said it with more affection than rancor, as if the teasing was part and parcel of their relationship.

"As if you could find me."

"If I could, you wouldn't be much use, would you? Everyone else on the planet would be knocking at your door to mount your head on the nearest pike." The prince chuckled and turned back to the group. "I hear there's a target out there."

"You hear correctly," Rod said. "In fact, the target is just across the street."

"That's stupid," Vernon said. "Didn't you tell us that this Norwegian Faction had a way to detect the BENT, often when even the subjects themselves didn't have a clue that they had a bend in the first place?"

"Yes. But in a city of more than six hundred thousand people, that won't make much difference. What are five more bends in a city full of them?" Rod said.

"Now that you mention it," Vernon said. "Where the hell are we?" He looked around the room. "I'm the only one who doesn't know, aren't I?"

"Yeah. But I said the coordinates in front of you," Rod chided. "Weren't you paying attention?"

"Yeah, like I can listen to a bunch of numbers and say, 'Yeah that's North Wilkesboro, North Carolina.' All I know for sure is that it's nighttime out there, and it was daytime when we left. Oh, and that street covered in snow makes me think it's probably cold as hell, too. If you brought us to Russia, I'm going to be annoyed. Do you have any idea how many Russians want to kill me?"

"Well, at least you're paying attention. This isn't Russia. It's Norway. Oslo, to be precise. And no one in the city knows we're here. Everyone in this group arrived through clandestine means, except for our royals who were invited on official business by the Stortinget."

Vernon wanted to ask what the hell a Stortinget was, but he didn't want to look like an imbecile in front of that amazingly beautiful princess, so he just nodded. "And the target is that big building there? Looks like a sports stadium, all covered in metal and taking up the whole block."

"It isn't. It's the head office of Jorgensen Pharmaceutical," Rod said.

Everyone in the room groaned.

"Isn't that a little too big a target to go after?" Maia asked.

"It's the target we need to hit. This isn't the place where the anti-BENT tech is being developed, but it's definitely the place where we'll find the information about that particular project. I need you to get me into the system and get out. Well, we also need to make it look like we wanted to steal something. So, after we infiltrate the system, we're going to grab one of Jorgensen's proto-AI SuperBrains."

"Surely you jest," the prince asked in tones that communicated supercilious incredulity.

"I never jest. And don't call me Shirley," Rod replied.

Everyone glared at the TV.

"Okay, I guess no one else thought that was funny. But I'm really not joking," Rod said. "We need to give them a big problem to think about instead of wondering what else we might have been doing in there. And that's the only one big enough. We grab a Brain and run for it, and Jorgensen won't even think of anything else." The Pooh Bear chuckled grotesquely. "If we grab the right Brain, they might not even be able to think about it."

"Sounds like a suicide mission," Maia said. "Security in there will likely be as tight as a virgin's a—" She glanced at the tall, elegant prince and stopped awkwardly. "Well, it will be tight. And the people and systems tasked with enforcing it are going to be well-armed. Specifically against the kind of people who can get inside in the first place. People like us."

"People *like* you," Rod replied. "But not exactly you. They'll be armed against super-strong BENTs, true. Which is why we won't send the royals into the Brain room for very long. And they'll be armed against teleporters, which is why you're not going to be doing the heavy lifting." The Pooh avatar smiled, showing teeth like a dinosaur. "The thing about defending against bends is that, if you don't know exactly what's coming, you can't really do anything about it but throw stuff at the wall and hope it sticks. Well, my research says that you guys can stop it from sticking."

Maia sighed. "And if you're wrong?"

"We're fucked," Rod said with an avatar's smile.

"*We're* fucked," Maia said. "You just need to recruit a new team and try again."

"If we fail, every BENT on the planet is dead. Maybe not today, maybe not tomorrow, but soon."

"You're just a fountain of old movie quotes today, aren't you?" the prince said. Then he looked around the room. "I knew the risks coming in, and I agreed to be a part of this. I'd like to get started as soon as possible."

"That's nice," Vernon said. "Except we didn't agree to anything. We just got dropped here on the assumption that we'd play along."

"And won't you?" Rod said. "Do you really want to spend the rest of your short lives wondering when a Faction goon is going to appear at your doorstep with their magic briefcase and melt you from your skin inward?"

"Damn you," Vernon said. "What's the plan?"

"We'll review your role, and that of the royals, in detail in a minute. First, though, we need Sarena to go in there and look around. She already knows what to do in the first phase of the op." The bear recited another spaghetti-string of numbers, and Maia nodded.

Sarena's clothes dropped to the floor, leaving nothing in their place but the suggestion of a breeze as she moved around the room.

Maia held out her hand and closed it around something unseen. A moment later, Maia blinked out of existence.

"Wait," Vernon said, an icy fist clutching his heart.

Before he could really worry about Maia, however, she reappeared. "All good," she reported. "I dropped Sarena in an empty corridor. I just hope you have the right codes for all those keypads. If not, I assume the place has all sorts of alarm-activated poison dust dispensers against people the security cameras can't see."

"She'll be fine," Rod replied. "Now, it's time to get the rest of you up to speed."

Chapter 6

Sarena shivered. Jorgensen Pharmaceuticals had decided, in their infinite wisdom, to turn the heat off at night. In the middle of winter. In Norway. Damn the Norwegians, anyway. Just like everyone else in Europe, they were stingy bastards when it came to energy. And water. Back home in Cairo, she never had to worry about freezing her ass off because she couldn't take her clothes with her when she went invisible.

And she could take long showers without bankrupting her entire family. And forget the stereotypes; no people on Earth smelled worse than middle-class Europeans.

Well, keep moving, then, she thought. *The sooner you get this done, the sooner you can do jumping jacks to keep warm.*

She approached the second door on the right, room 407, and punched in the code she'd memorized. 1219.

Then she held her breath and hoped for the best. If the alarms went off, it would be the shortest covert operation ever.

And the only person who would take the fall for it would be Sarena. The rest of the team would—with help from that teleporter woman—disappear at the first sign of commotion. While the Norwegian cops tossed her in a cell that could conceivably be even colder than the office building, they'd be on a beach in some tropical paradise sipping drinks with umbrellas in them.

The lock clicked, and she opened the door. Alarms failed to sound.

Good. She walked inside and closed the door behind her.

This room had a little bit of light, which came from a small desk lamp they probably kept on so the guards could make an occasional inspection. Other than that, the room was a typical office space. The outer walls held four executive offices, which, even in the dim light, she could see were cavernous, with large desks and little meeting tables surrounded by chairs.

The enormous offices surrounded what could only be called a cube farm, a workspace for nine people packed into a space no larger than one of the offices. They didn't even have privacy; the cubicle walls were barely taller than her waist.

So much for European egalitarianism, she thought. The more she was exposed to the hypocrisies of European society, the more she pined for home. *We might be mostly poor, but at least we're honest about it. Here, the rich pretend not to be ostentatious, and the poor . . . Well, I actually think the poor believe they're somehow close to the rich. And that's just stupid.*

And though the executives in those offices might be decision makers, there was only one truly important computer terminal in this office. That was a laptop that sat on a desk that was on the right hand position of the middle row of the three by three grid of cubicles. And it was connected to a secure subnet of the Jorgensen system.

She strode to it quickly and then stopped dead in her tracks. Someone was working the door.

Sarena didn't panic. Over the past six years—her bend had manifested when she was thirteen—she'd found herself invisible in countless places she shouldn't have been, places where, if she'd been discovered, she would have been punished. In fact, most of the places she'd infiltrated had been the lairs of the kind of people who wouldn't turn over a teenaged burglar to the police. They would make you disappear, and you'd spend any time that elapsed between the moment they caught you and the moment you died wishing they'd finish you off fast.

So, a security guard in a Norwegian office building wasn't going to make her panic.

She still preferred not to get caught, so the first thing to do was to get herself behind a cubicle wall. If the doofus had IR, he could see her, but not if she was blocked by a cloth-covered partition. And the second thing to do was to hold her breath. She was sure it was cold enough in this stupid office that the condensation from her exhalations would be visible.

Sarena ducked behind the outer wall of one of the rows, which was carpeted in the same light color—she thought it was gray, but it was hard to tell in the dim light—as the rest of the room.

Just look inside and get on with the next office, she thought at the guard.

Unfortunately, her bend wasn't telepathy, and it *definitely* wasn't the kind of telepathy that actually convinced people to do things. Even worse, the guard apparently was one of those weirdos who thought they had to do their job to the best of their ability, even if they were being paid less than a dog on a TV show.

He actually began to walk around the perimeter of the room, shining his light into the offices. Fortunately, he didn't appear to be wearing an IR headset, which meant he didn't suspect there had been an incursion. Which, in turn, meant that Rod's info about the place where the cameras wouldn't be able to see them enter—the teleport woman was fully visible—were correct.

She would have felt a hell of a lot better at this demonstration of Rod's competence were it not for the fact that the guard had rounded the corner of the cubicle farm, and she could see him: a rotund blond man with a flashlight and a gray uniform. Was the corridor between the cubes and the offices wide enough that he wouldn't trip over her? Or, just as bad, that he wouldn't feel the heat from her naked body?

Sarena didn't think so. She began to crawl, slowly, silently, in the direction of the next row of cubicles where a little passageway allowed the employees to slip into their workstations.

Her breath burned as she held it, and it was all she could do not to breathe out explosively. Every nerve in her body wanted to move faster, but a slow crawl was all she dared risk.

The guard had stopped to shine his light through the window of the next office. The man was quite conscientious, damn him.

When he started toward her again, Sarena was still half a meter away from the passage she was aiming for. She had to force herself to put one hand in front of the other and not dive noisily for the gap.

Her lungs screamed for mercy.

But she made herself go slowly, to avoid making noise at any cost.

The man's flashlight bean shone right through her.

Then it went away, pointing in a different direction, and Sarena finally managed to turn the corner and creep under one of the desks.

She let her breath out slowly. It was pure torture that lasted until she could breathe in again.

The guard walked past, completed his circuit of the room, and left using the same door he'd entered through.

Sarena sighed with relief and worked to get her respiration back to normal. All she managed was a hiccough.

Damn, she thought. Wouldn't that be a stupid way to get caught and killed? A security mic recognizes a hiccough as an unexpected sound.

Carefully, slowly, she crawled out from under the desk and got her bearings. The laptop she wanted was . . . that one.

Sarena gritted her teeth as she opened the lid. Rod had promised that there were no motion detectors in the room, and logically, had there been, the act of opening the door would have set them off. Still, it was her ass in a sling if that Disney-obsessed hacker got it wrong.

The password prompt came up, and she typed the word she'd memorized: *Yllan$tano22*. Probably a woman's desk, then. Yllan Stano was a heartthrob, an actor Uzbekistan who dominated the Asian box office. His bend, the legend had it, was to exude an air of irresistibility to women, even through the screen.

Sarena had never bought it. The movies she'd seen of him had been fine, but she definitely didn't feel he was one of those 'there wasn't a dry seat in the house' matinee idols. Maybe his bend just didn't work on her. He was good-looking, but others pushed her buttons more effectively.

The welcome screen opened, and Sarena got to work. Her job was almost ridiculously easy: open a browser tab, enter a web address that Rod had given her, download a file. She waited for the download to be complete and then counted to ten. That was the time Rod's program needed in order to finish the job and erase any traces of its presence.

Then she simply closed the laptop, left the office through the door, and walked back to the spot where their teleport BENT had dropped her.

Now, all she could do was to wait and wonder about why a group of evil plotters would allow a menial-level worker access to the backend. Probably because the evil plot side of Jorgensen Pharmaceuticals generated a ton of paperwork, and none of the senior evildoers could be bothered to file and organize it.

Why, after all, would the leaders of evil projects be any different to the ones who ran normal, everyday companies? This time, though, they would pay for their laziness.

Shivering, Sarena watched her breath hang in the air, and tried to will Maia to hurry up.

All she managed was to remind herself that she still wasn't telepathic.

"You mean all of us are just a diversion?" Vernon asked, gesturing to the people in the room. "That Sarena has already done what we came here to do? And that what we're about to pull is just a sideshow?"

"A hugely important part of the mission," Rod replied. One of the advantages he had in hiding behind an avatar—and most likely a voice-modification program as well—was that he could pretend to remain calm no matter how many times he had to repeat himself. "Look, we went in as clean as I could manage. Maia won't appear on security tapes, and Sarena is invisible. But at some point, someone is going to push tonight's data through analysis software, and they'll find a couple of anomalies. Doors that open to admit no one, a laptop that opens its own lid. Temperature fluctuations where they shouldn't be. It might not be a top priority, but it will get to the front of the security check line eventually, that's just the way things are. But if a huge, obvious incursion happens on the same night, the security geeks will either miss the small stuff entirely or assume we had a teleporter and a ghost clearing the path before the main assault." He paused, and the avatar's ink-black eyes looked at Vernon. How two dots could peer into your soul and make you feel like you were being weighed and measured, Vernon didn't know. But that was what these dots were doing. "We can't do this part of the mission without you. And if we don't do it, then the whole mission will fail. The Norwegian Faction will know one of their computers was compromised, and they'll relocate their center of operations before we can track it. Sarena's risk will be for naught. We're counting on you."

"Fuck," Vernon said. He took hold of Maia's hand.

Chapter 7

Alarms sounded almost before they finished materializing in the lab. Bright white lights illuminated the space, the kind of cold illumination Vernon associated with hospitals.

A guard ran toward them. This wasn't some rent-a-cop security guard, but a guy with short-cropped blond hair that looked like he should be making airborne drops over enemy territory at night. His white-and-gray camo uniform made him look like he'd just come in from mountain assault exercises.

The guard pulled a serious-looking submachine gun from a black utility belt and raised it. He said something in what Vernon assumed must have been Norwegian. It sounded like a drunken and angry German man saying things that were almost intelligible to an English speaker.

The royals didn't hesitate. Hand in hand, they charged the soldier, who proceeded to empty a magazine into them.

Vernon heard the bullets drop onto the floor after they spent themselves against the prince and princess. A moment later, the prince used his free hand to grab the guard by the arm and tossed him, spinning wildly, into a wall at bone-breaking speed.

The man fell limply to the floor.

Other guards shouted in the distance—the subterranean lab appeared to have a much larger footprint than the office building visible from the street.

"Will you two stop playing around and open the door? Then you can all get the hell out of here," Vernon said.

The door in question was a thick metal screen that cordoned off a chunk of square floorspace thirty feet high and about fifty feet to a side. Vernon's skin could have burned a hole in it, but it would have taken some time.

The royals attacked it with vigor. They moved in unison, never letting go of each other's hands. It was a beautiful thing to watch, like Olympic figure skating or synchronized swimming. Except that the result of their beautifully choreographed artistry was a torn and broken curtain wall, torn asunder in seconds.

Vernon listened. A hissing sound coming from the roof told him all he needed to know. "Good. Now get the hell out of here. They've started gassing us."

The royals grabbed Maia, and all three of them disappeared.

A yellowish mist began to float down from the roof. Vernon idly wondered what it might be. Probably some hyper-corrosive nerve agent. Or a cloud of acid. Something nasty, in any event. Something you couldn't teleport into or defeat with super strength alone.

He closed his eyes and pulled a pair of goggles from his pocket. The lenses were glass, and they fit snugly—extremely snugly—over his eyes. Then he plugged his ears and nose.

Now, I just need to remember to keep my mouth shut, he thought.

That was easy enough to remember. After walking underwater for so long, it was almost second nature. His skin would diffuse the necessary oxygen out of the ambient gas. As long as there was even a trace of oxygen around—even if it was mixed up in hyper-poisonous concoctions—he would be fine.

The guards, on the other hand, were not fine. Though two of the men approaching him had managed to get gas hoods over their heads, one of them was struggling to close the strap. As Vernon watched, he released the hood and took his hands to his eyes. Then, forgetting himself completely, he screamed like a terrified horse and ran as fast as he could toward a door. He never made it. His eyes must have been completely destroyed by whatever the evil green mist was, because he slammed into something that looked like an enormous upright microscope. Glass shattered, and he fell in a heap, the heavy metal of the equipment overbalancing onto him.

The other guards opened fire. Vernon turned away from them. The only part of his body at risk were the goggles. A bullet would shatter them—and possibly even harm his unprotected eyes. That could mess up his entire day.

He felt the impacts of the bullets on his skin. The chemical destruction of the projectiles was nearly instantaneous . . . but just a tiny amount of the kinetic energy and momentum was transmitted through the clothes he wore.

He smiled, but then frowned. He should have been under a consistent hail of fire, but five seconds had passed since the last bullet hit him in the back—meaning he'd have to replace yet another set of clothes.

Vernon turned to see what was up with the guards.

They were lying on their backs, twitching, every centimeter of exposed skin bubbling like a cauldron. As bubbles burst, blood poured out, to begin, in turn, bubbling madly.

Nasty indeed, he thought, and made a mental note never to send his résumé to Jorgensen Pharmaceuticals.

He stepped through the wreckage of the curtain wall to find a glass door. It only had a handle, no sophisticated security, so he opened it and stepped through into a square room that must have served as a species of airlock. The next door opened after five seconds, in which fans replaced the contaminated air from outside with pure air from somewhere unseen. The walls of this room were glass, and the gas wasn't getting in. Still, he left the goggles on.

The cold hit him for just a second before his skin found an exothermic reaction it could run to keep him warm using just the elements in the purified air around him. How nitrogen and oxygen could be burned for heat was beyond Vernon, but he was used to the operation by now.

He breathed out, just to see what would happen, and quickly closed his mouth as his breath hung in the air. It was really, really cold in there.

Five pools filled with bright-blue liquid dotted the square enclosure. From each, a tangle of black cables, covered in frost, emerged to snake across the floor and bury themselves in banks of computer equipment.

Vernon knew he didn't have a lot of time. He was hard to damage, sure, but not impossible. Concussion waves—like that from a nearby explosion—would fuck him up. So would large amounts of hard radiation, or even well-concentrated microwaves. If the people gunning for him managed to recognize his weaknesses, he was as good as dead.

He grinned.

Fortunately, using any of those methods in this room would destroy at least one SuperBrain, probably all five of them.

He peered into the nearest of the pools. The cryogenic fluid, whatever it was, was liquid, unfrozen. *Some kind of super-duty electrolytic antifreeze,* he thought to himself. Then he chuckled. He didn't even know what any of those words meant, chemically speaking.

The brains in there were cold.

And he had to grab one.

The easiest way would probably be to reach in and grasp the place where all the cables came together. Vernon really didn't want to do that, so he did what Rod had instructed him to do: he pulled on the black cable.

His skin must have compensated to keep the cold off, because the cable melted a little each time he put his hands around it. Slowly, as if trying to pull a rope through cold maple syrup, the node where all the cables joined together came closer to the edge.

The liquid didn't stick to the cable, fortunately. It stretched slightly as any given section of wire came out of the pool, only to fall immediately back in.

A superfluid, he thought, wondering what the hell such a thing might be.

Finally, he managed to grab hold of the large, heavy mass of cables and began to disengage the largest ones. They were held in place by strong screw-tightened bolts. No matter, he simply squeezed the joins between his fingers, and they dissolved in moments.

When the big cables were gone, he was left with a cylinder about the size of a can of Campbell's soup with a bunch of smaller tendril cables emerging from it. He pulled at them, and they came off. Perhaps no quicker than melting them with his power, but infinitely more satisfying.

He glanced out of the glass cube to see that the first space he'd entered, the large lab area, was now completely opaque with green mist. That made it unlikely that anyone would be in there, so he checked his goggles and headed back out.

The mist was so thick, he imagined he would have to swim through it, but he knew that was most likely just because his skin was creating something to neutralize the chemicals in the air. Vernon felt the activity as a warm glow of the epidermis.

Keeping his mouth firmly shut, he sprinted toward the wall opposite where they'd entered. It was an interesting run, since objects had a way of appearing out of the corrosive murk at unexpected intervals, and he had to swerve to avoid hitting them. Still, the risk of his hosts figuring out what his bend was and finding a way to neutralize it was greater than that of running into something.

So, he ran.

He'd never known how it felt to be out of breath. He was never out of breath. Somehow, even when he was breathing through his mouth, his skin found a way to feed oxygen straight into his bloodstream. It made him great at track, and made him the best underwater swimmer ever. It also made running through a gas chamber a walk in the park.

Finally, he reached a wall.

This wasn't a problem. It was an opportunity. He pressed against the poured concrete, and it gave way around him, albeit not as quickly as he would have liked. He spent several tense moments melting his way through the wall before he was deep enough for concealment. Once there, he turned and sealed the wall behind him—his bend taking his desire to not be followed and interpreting it as the need to create a new wall. It wasn't airtight, but with luck, no one would notice that one sector of the room looked different from the rest until he was long gone.

Now he stopped and looked around. He was in a maintenance tunnel that must have run next to the lab wall, which was much better than the alternative, which would have been to attempt to use his skin to tunnel through a few hundred meters of dirt. He was sure he could have managed it, but he wasn't certain how the chemical factory would do such a thing.

Not understanding his skin's action was his way of putting his head in the sand, and he knew it. He wanted to go through life blithely believing he could do anything he set his mind to as long as he didn't know how it was done.

Someday, his ignorance was going to get him killed.

But it looked like today was not going to be that day.

Vernon ran down the corridor—mouth still closed against the near-certainty of poison gas leaking through the hole he'd made—in the direction opposite where most of the action had occurred. Or at least as well as he could estimate said direction while running through an underground tunnel.

He came to a stairwell and sprinted up the staircase, not bothering to try to figure out where he was. Up was up, and that was the direction he needed. Three floors later, the stairs ended at a steel door. He tried to open it, but the door refused to budge. So, he simply stepped forward, dissolving the door as he went.

Unfortunately, whatever his skin did to the door also melted his clothes away. The only thing that didn't get atomized was the little canister that held the Brain. Rod had told him that, if he couldn't capture a Brain, destroying it was almost as good, but it was a question of pride to complete the mission as designed, so Vernon had made certain to leave the hand holding the canister behind the rest of his body until he was certain that the hole through which he would pass wouldn't close up to just the size of his hand.

As usual, his skin had anticipated the need and made it happen.

So, there he stood, stark naked, in a long, bright hallway in which alarms were screeching, lights flashing—both red and blue, whatever that might mean—and where, in the distance, a golf cart filled with white-coated people scrambled.

The place looked like an airport, but he knew it was the main entrance hall to the Jorgensen building.

Windows faced the street outside. He was in luck: their midwinter assault in northern latitudes meant the night was long, so it was still dark outside, without even the rosy glow of impending dawn.

A quick push on the glass melted it away, and he stepped into the street.

Freshly fallen snow melted as his feet landed in it, and the air steamed away from his body. He didn't stop to wonder if his miraculous skin might get overworked; he'd put it under a lot more stress than this, and it hadn't let him down yet.

Vernon stuck to the shadows, but there were few people out and about. It made sense; midwinter before sunrise on the streets of Oslo was not a place you wanted to be.

The first order of business was to get away from the vicinity of the lab. He walked several blocks—nearly scaring the life out of an old woman walking a tiny dog—before setting sight on the second objective: finding a surveillance camera.

Finally, he located one on a lamppost. A round excrescence too high up for the criminal element of the city to disable. He simply stood there in full view of it for a few minutes.

He wasn't concerned about the cops. Any security forces who saw him standing naked on the street would be more likely to send help than lethal force; this was Norway, after all. He just hoped Rod was as good as he claimed to be.

A moment later, his faith was justified. Maia appeared out of thin air, looked him up and down with a smirk that disappeared as she scanned him.

"Hell"—she pouted, eyebrow raised as she looked at his crotch—"you don't look as cold as I expected you to. That's no fun."

Then she put her hand on his arm, and they blinked away.

Chapter 8

The man who called himself Lars had a real name, but it was buried so deep in false identities that he almost couldn't remember it. He'd been eighteen, a first-year university student in Belgium, when he'd had his first contact with the Norwegian Factor.

Of course, the Factor had also changed names since then. Back then, it called itself Reaction Directe, an homage to Action Directe, a French revolutionary group from the 1970s. Like its forebear, this was a left-wing group that defended the rights of people it saw as victims of the system. Unlike its forebear, this group specifically included the economic hegemony that inevitably would come through the existence of humans who had powers that others couldn't even begin to imagine, much less match: the BENT.

At first, only Talents, those BENT who could actually use their powers to make a large impression, were targeted. But soon, the arguments over where to draw the line became a threat to the group's existence. As in every revolutionary group, each individual pushed for the line to be drawn just above them. In much the same way as worker's group members wanted everyone richer than themselves to be excluded, in Reaction Directe, every member with a bend wanted the next guy up the ladder to be bounced.

Finally, the group leadership decided that there was no line to be drawn. All BENT were expelled, even those with trivial powers.

Ironically, it was this drastic move that created a spike in membership. The radical action against the BENT proved attractive to those who truly felt excluded. People with little prospect of success, people with strong obsessions and persecution complexes. In short, the kind of people who could be counted on to do the dirty work that a group like Reaction Directe needed to do if it was to advance its cause. Expendable people.

Lars had never been one of them.

But one of his girlfriends, more a fuck-buddy than a real relationship, was. Veronika was into every radical idea that the Faculty of Philosophy threw her way. That included a stint with Reaction Directe, during which she was completely subsumed by some of their sillier ideas. She went well beyond the usual peaceful protests and being a civil nuisance, to the point where she actually got tossed in jail for it.

A couple of weeks in the clink convinced her that the revolutionary life was better suited to other people, and she left for a career in journalism—and Lars lost track of her—but Lars had seen enough of her material, and met enough of her friends, to be intrigued.

He joined Reaction Directe not as cannon fodder but as a junior member of the committee for college recruitment all across Benelux, a fertile ground for bored and otherwise unproductive young idealists.

Lars quickly achieved a position of trust, and as the group's membership spread northward into Germany and Scandinavia, he moved into the Norwegian Faction, a subgroup that eventually took over the whole shooting match.

But even though he'd grown to become one of the most trusted members of the organization, privy to secrets and with a good working knowledge of where the bodies were buried, Lars had never liked to sit behind a desk. He wanted to be out in the field working directly against the enemies of humanity. He wanted to be bribing politicians to get laws passed, recruiting CEOs so they would cleanse their workforces of people with unfair advantages, and, when possible, killing the BENT.

That meant he'd gone through a complete telephone directory of false names and fake occupations. He'd been a director of sales, a meteorologist, a college swim coach, an art history professor. He changed names and addresses twice a month. He was sometimes married—and the Faction would supply a suitable member for the charade—sometimes single. Sometimes gay and sometimes straight. He'd had a half-dozen operations on the bone structure in his face, and his eyes had changed color permanently. Now, he had depilated his head.

He must have had a hundred names, and in each of those roles, he'd been convincing enough to get the job done.

So, when his phone—the phone he'd been handed with the rest of the material he'd need to do his work in Los Angeles—rang and the voice on the other end said: "Hello, Thierry, it's been a long time since Antwerp," his blood froze. Thierry was the name he'd been born with, a moniker he'd never thought to hear again.

"Who is this?" he managed to choke out after a second.

"Someone who wants to talk to you," the voice replied.

"Who?"

"The less you know, the better." Now the voice held a chiding tone. "I think you should know that by now."

"No."

Lars disconnected the call and walked to his car. He knew the caller would call back—no one who'd gone to the effort of tracking him down would give up that easily—but he needed time to think. He drove to the expressway and headed east. He wanted to get to Las Vegas before nightfall. That was where his new identity awaited.

Halfway across the Mojave desert, he finally relented and answered the call.

"All right," he said tersely. "Either you tell me who you are and what you want, or I'll just toss this phone out the window, and you'll have to look for me again. If you keep tracking me after that, I'll get a desk job under my original name so any value I might have to you as a field agent will be gone."

That earned him a moment's hesitation from the person on the other end of the line. "Very well," the voice said finally. "My name is Khi Bord, and I don't want anything from you. What I do want is to tell you who was responsible for the break-in at Jorgensen Pharmaceuticals last night."

"How did you . . ."

He was about to ask how the voice even knew about that, when he'd only heard from the Committee that morning. If he'd needed any further evidence that the caller was legitimate, this was it.

"It was incidental. An old enemy of the organization I work with—a person I've been tracking for months and who I had under surveillance, happened to be in Oslo. This person—whom I will not name—became involved with what I can only describe as a BENT task force with extremely advanced tech support."

"You're talking to the wrong person," Lars said. "Jorgensen is only a partner for our operations, not a central player. You need to talk to their CEO."

"Most people would believe you when you say that, but we both know that Jorgensen's supercomputers are the tactical heart of the Norwegian Faction."

Lars was silent for a moment. Very, very few people—in Jorgensen or in the Faction—knew that. He was treading on extremely dangerous ground. "You still have the wrong person. You should go to the Committee. If you have the resources and contacts to track my movements, I'm sure you know exactly how to reach them."

"Of course. I have most of them on speed dial. The only problem is that I have no interest in reaching the Committee. I want to talk to you, not them. You have ten seconds to tell me whether you're interested in what I have to say. If you are, we need to meet in person. I'm not going to speak over the cellular network."

Lars hesitated for only half the allotted time before answering. "Yes. I'll meet."

It wasn't like he had any real choice in the matter.

"Good. I'll call you back. Try not to lose this phone when you change identities again. I'd be annoyed if I had to go to the effort of tracking you back down."

"Disgusting, isn't it?" The old man at the table must have been in his late seventies. Thin silver hair topped a head covered in liver spots and moles. His skin was tanned and his nose just slightly crooked, and his voice had decades of whisky imprinted on it. "I can remember a day when the strippers were real, not mutants."

His actions, however, belied his words; he was staring at the woman on stage just the way men had stared, fascinated, at naked, sexualized women since time began.

The dancer had stopped gyrating around the pole to pout, G-string full of dollar bills, at the crowd. Her bare breasts got bigger . . . and bigger. They looked like they would burst, but still got bigger. Despite the size, gravity appeared to hold no sway over the fantastic orbs.

Lars tore his eyes from the woman. "You're not the man I spoke to earlier."

"Of course not. I'm just a hired lackey. The man you spoke to has no intention of being identified or even possibly being put at risk by talking to you. And I enjoy these little missions, especially since I have enough money on me to enjoy the view"— he nodded at the woman he'd called disgusting just moments before—"and to drink until I drop. Perks of the assignment."

"So, why should I talk to you?"

"Because I have the information you need."

Lars snorted. "Are you sure you can remember it all, old man?"

"Not a lot to remember, really. You have questions. The first question you've got is how my employer found you. That, I can't answer, because, to me, the guy is just a distorted voice on voice chats originating from unknown numbers. Your other question is how we're supposed to be able to help you. *That*, I can answer."

Lars clenched and unclenched his hands. In the dim light of the seating area, the man's neck looked particularly easy to break. He took a deep breath. He wouldn't learn anything if he gave in to his irritation.

"All right. I'd love to hear it," Lars replied.

"As you probably know, they stole one of your supercomputers."

"Not mine. They belong to Jorgensen Pharmaceutical."

The old man shrugged. "Do you want to hear this or not? Do you think I care who owns what? I'm just a messenger. I get paid to deliver messages."

"Yes. We know they have the Brain."

"All right, then here's the message: they're planning to use the Brain to track the Committee of the Norwegian Faction through their connections with Jorgensen Pharmaceutical. The plan is to identify the top movers, track their movements, and assassinate them all on one specific night." The old man looked Lars up and down. "Does that make more sense to you than it does to me?"

Lars nodded. "Perfect sense, though I don't see how . . ."

The man held up a hand. "I can't answer questions, and I don't want to know any of the context around this. Besides, I have a second part of the message to deliver."

"I'm listening," Lars said grimly.

"The team they'll use is composed of one woman with an invisibility bend, a super-strength unit, and a guy who is pretty much impervious to any direct physical assault. Plus a transport, a teleport." The old man cleared his throat. "That's it. That's the message."

Lars nodded. "It makes sense. That team—"

The messenger held up his hands. "I told you already. I really, really don't want to know. And by that, I mean I don't want to know anything about what happened, where it happened, or why it happened. I've said my bit, and I get paid for the risk I took. If you go around blurting crap I'm not supposed to know, my risk goes up." The old man raised his red eyes to meet Lars's gaze. "And I'm not being paid enough for that."

"I understand," Lars replied tersely.

"Good, so unless you're prepared to help me in the task of watching that young woman over there inflate and deflate to the beat, I'd suggest you find somewhere else to be."

"Very well. Thank you for the message."

"You're welcome."

Lars left the man staring at the woman with the pornographic bend while another performer danced onto the stage. This one was dressed in a skirt and a T-shirt, but her whole body glowed so you could see what was inside.

The crowd howled.

Lars shook his head and left the club, thinking that the description of the assault team matched the report from the attack in Oslo.

Would they really try to hit the Committee?

Could they, with the information they'd gotten?

The main question, however, was why come to Lars with the warning? He saw no reason they couldn't go straight to the Committee with this.

Something wasn't right.

But that didn't mean he could sit on the warning. Lars sighed and pulled out his phone.

Chapter 9

"I'm worried," Vernon said.

They sat on the bed in a hotel room in Cartagena, Colombia. A cutesy-rustic circular cabin with a thatched roof and a completely inappropriate South Seas vibe. Nothing in the colonial Caribbean had ever looked that way, but apparently, the proprietors of the hotel didn't care.

They also didn't seem to have done much checking on the payment origin and accepted whatever stolen credit card Rod had supplied the team with without blinking. They'd been received like visiting royalty.

"What is there to worry about?" Maia asked. "I mean, sure, we're on the run from a vicious criminal organization"—she grinned—"but we're always on the run from vicious criminal organizations. That's kind of like our jam."

"That's not what I'm worried about." He shook his head, knowing Maia was going to laugh. He didn't care. "I'm worried about those computer geeks."

Maia cocked her head. "What about them?"

"Did you see how they laughed as they worked on that SuperBrain? And the jokes they told? It was . . ." He hesitated. "You're going to laugh. But it reminded me of that movie about the Pinochet dictatorship."

"What are you talking about? First off, I never watch crap like that. Secondly, it sounds like one of those films made by 'brave'"—she made air quotes—"left-wing moviemakers twenty years after the threat of getting arrested is gone. I don't care about politics, and I especially don't care about political films made by some smug millionaire pretending to be a guerilla while sitting in his Hollywood mansion."

"There's a scene in this movie in which a bunch of military doctors are torturing a woman in an illegal detention center. They've beaten her up and put cigarettes out on her face and given her electric shocks when one of them wonders if they could make her have an orgasm even if she didn't want to, just by some sort of stimulation. That guy was actually perfectly serious, the actor played it for scientific curiosity. But the other three—including one doctor who was a woman—were sadistic, and they laughed and took bets. And I know they were just actors, but the guys working on that computer reminded me of those three doctors. It's not like they're trying to pull information, but more like they're enjoying a torture session." He looked away, knowing that Maia, who knew a hell of a lot more about technology than he did, would be mocking him in 3 . . . 2 . . . 1 . . .

She remained silent for a few moments, prolonging his anguish.

"Fuck," she said finally. "Just try not to think about it, okay?"

"What does that even mean?"

"Exactly what I said. We're in deep enough without you antagonizing our allies," Maia said. "Just leave it alone. Come on."

She took him by the hand, and he braced to teleport somewhere, but instead, she pulled him out the door and into the little courtyard encircled by five identical cottages. Glaring sunshine descended from a deep blue sky and reflected off the white sand on the beach just fifty feet away.

Despite his misgivings, Vernon felt himself relaxing. The sight of people playing volleyball nearby and the turquoise Caribbean, so serene, calmed him in spite of himself.

"Oh, look," Maia said. "The royals are over there."

"Good," he replied cattily, "I've been meaning to ask the princess her real name. I can't just call her 'Your Highness' the rest of our lives, can I?"

"Do you think there will be rest of your life with her? Dream on."

"And you and the prince?" he shot back.

They glared at each other for a minute before Maia laughed. "Look at us," she said.

Vernon felt his anger dissolving into a grin. "Yeah. Why would either of those even look at us twice? We're just normal people."

Maia put her hand on his arm. "Actually, you're not that bad," she said with a smile. Then she winked to let him know what, specifically, she was talking about.

"And you look amazing. Any guy who doesn't look twice at you is missing something."

She smiled. "Yeah, and besides, those two are much too pretty to be any good in bed."

"Want to go back inside?"

"Lets."

For a fleeting moment, he wondered if Maia had orchestrated the lightning-quick fight and make up to take his mind off . . .

. . . He couldn't actually remember what he'd been worried about, which made him grin. If that was the case, she'd proven once again that she was smarter than he was.

"Antarctica?" Vernon asked. "What is it with these people and places where you freeze your butt off?"

"They're Norwegian," the laptop with the Pooh Bear image on it responded. "They like cold places." They were in a small meeting room that the hotel rented out for conferences and lent to guests as part of their stay.

"But that's just stupid," Maia replied. "Anyone doing anything in Antarctica would be located immediately. There's almost nothing going on in Antarctica, and every major power has a satellite looking down on it."

"Well, that's where the Faction has their base," Rod replied. "And we have to find a way to get in."

"Easy. Just drop the same strike team as we did to get the Brain. Can the defenses be any better than they were in the headquarters of Jorgensen Pharmaceuticals? I did a little digging after our jaunt in there, and they spent billions on that setup. Of course, most of the defenses were designed to keep us from actually getting into the main room in the first place—which meant they were behind us by the time we released Vern in there, but they were impressive."

"More than that," the prince said, "they were hyper-lethal. Some of that gas got out through the hole Vernon made in the walls and killed four passersby. That chemical soup was extremely deadly, and it would have definitely gotten my sister and I, as well as Maia, if we'd stayed behind. Super-strength stuff."

"So, is Jorgensen going to get sued out of business now?" Sarena asked.

Maia and Vernon exchanged a look that said *Sweet summer child, how much you still have to learn*, but said nothing.

Rod wasn't quite as tactful. "I thought you were born nineteen years ago, not yesterday? Jorgensen is Norway's biggest tax-money generator after the oil industry, and the Norwegian government basically spends most of the GDP on bread-and-circus type programs to make sure no one is poor, not even the dumbest or laziest citizens in their society. Jorgensen's C-suite execs could go on a chainsaw spree in a shopping mall, and they still wouldn't be punished." The bear's eyes grew wide. "Oh, I'm sure they'll levy a fine and pay a little hush money to the families, but Jorgensen isn't going anywhere."

Sarena sat back in her seat, eyes downcast.

"What Maia suggested would be a good idea," Rod continued, "except we have no idea where they built the facility."

"Again," Maia insisted, "there's no way they could build anything in Antarctica without the world knowing about it. Surely there has to be one country whose spy satellite security is weak enough for you to break into."

Steam came out of the bear's ears. Rod must have spent quite a lot of time making the avatar interactive. Vernon imagined him sitting in a basement somewhere—not his mother's, a hacker like him would be much too rich to live with his parents—surrounded by computer equipment, and with way too much time on his hands.

"I'll have you know," the bear said, "that I can access every single spy satellite control system on the planet, even the ones that aren't connected to the public internet. The operation Sarena executed in Oslo wasn't the first time I've used that method.

I can also pretty much listen in to everything happening on the NSA's network, and the CIA's morning briefings are open on my machine as soon as the analyst in charge finishes composing them. The same with the Russian and Chinese versions. The reason I haven't seen the construction is that it wasn't visible from the air."

"Then it didn't happen," Maia said.

"Then it happened, but the bastards used BENT to do it," Vernon replied. "Think about it. A few teleporters is all you really need, as long as they can transport the necessary machinery."

"Full marks to Mr. Pandor," Rod said. "Once the heavy work is done, they use a disguised tunnel to get in and out, waiting for the windows when satellites aren't overhead. Which is pretty easy, as there's only token surveillance of places in which none of the powers are doing anything significant."

"And they killed the teleporters," Maia said.

"Of course. They were too risky to keep around, so they probably just had them shot in the back when they weren't looking. After all, you can always find another teleporting BENT, but you can't move the entire Antarctic facility if one of them blabs."

"So much for the purity of the human race," the princess said with a sneer. "These guys can't even build their genocide lab without help from the BENT. Can you imagine how fast their entire world would fall apart if they actually did manage to kill us off?"

"There's plenty of history of people using slave labor from groups they meant to kill off," Rod said. "And we shouldn't get too full of ourselves. After all, baseline humans managed to survive throughout all of history without BENT help."

"Well, I don't plan on letting them get used to it again," Sarena said. Her face was flushed.

"That's the spirit," the Pooh Bear avatar said. "But we can't actually act on the information we currently have." He gestured to Maia. "We can't teleport underground without precise coordinates. And we can't just make our best guess. That's a good way to be entombed in ice for future generations to find and puzzle about."

"Doesn't the Brain know?" Vernon asked.

Rod hesitated. It was just a second, but enough to be noticeable. "No. We asked, but it confirmed what I already suspected. The Jorgensen people are being kept out of the loop about the main operation. They're only involved in the normal, day-to-day terrorism the group performs. And that, only on the financial side. They're sponsors, not operatives. I tracked the money to figure out about Antarctica. Purchases and such."

"Well, that's good, anyway. At least the Antarctic facility won't have a SuperBrain coordinating its defenses," Maia said.

"The lab didn't either. If it had, we would never have been able to slip through the cracks," Rod replied. "I'm pretty sure the next team to try to get through won't be so lucky."

"As long as it isn't me again," Vernon said, "I couldn't care less."

"But the question remains about how we're going to go about finding a single underground facility in a place that's both enormous and hostile to life," Rod said.

"Why don't you take over one of NASA's ground penetrating radar satellites?" Maia asked.

"Because those are orbiting Mars, which won't help much," Rod replied. "Well, technically, there's one in the northern hemisphere, but we'd need to move it over the spot where we want. Want to go up there and push it into polar orbit for me?"

Maia wrinkled her nose. "I don't deal well with vacuum. Do you have a spacesuit?"

"That might not be a bad idea," Rod replied. "Steal it and teleport it into place. But I was thinking maybe expanding the crew a bit instead. I was thinking of getting someone to help us out."

"Since when have you ever asked us our opinion on that?" Vernon said. "Hell, I never even agreed to do the stuff I already did."

"This time, I need you guys to give me your okay, because the BENT I want to add to the crew is Eyespy," Rod said.

"Right," Maia replied. "So, where do we go about finding a spacesuit? I'm sure NASA has plenty of EVA suits we can steal. And you should go about trying to hack into this satellite's systems."

"Hear me out. I actually think recruiting Eyespy is a better idea."

"Nothing having to do with Eyespy is a good idea. The man is a psychopath, a murderer, and a loose cannon. Worse, he's creepy. Let him rot in jail."

"They have him in The Hole," Rod said. "No one deserves that."

"Oh, I can think of a few. And Eyespy is near the top of that list. And even if you could spring him, you can't control him. Which is why they created The Hole in the first place." Maia looked around the table. "People like Eyespy need to be locked up."

"Wow," the prince said. "You really don't seem to like this guy. Care to fill us in? I know he can do weird stuff with his eyes . . . but that's it. What does he do? Look through women's clothes with his x-ray vision?"

"Hah. I'd have been fine with that," Maia said. "Hell, I personally know a lot of BENTs who are seriously more deviant than that would be. But that's just the start of his creepiness. He can record what he sees. And he can see through houses. There was a time when half the porn in Russia was recordings of regular couples in their own apartments who didn't know he was standing outside in the hall. That's how he made his first fortune." Maia took a breath. "But even that isn't why I hate him. I hate him because he can use any kind of electromagnetic rays—and some really exotic stuff like neutrino streams—to look through things. The problem is that he can also use those same rays to give you cancer or burn out your insides. He might be standing on the other side of the world when he did it, too. His second fortune was in snuff films. People being microwaved from the inside out while he recorded it." She grunted. "The Mafia hired him as an assassin, and he even sold some of those videos—which is how he got in trouble."

"And how do you know all this?" the prince asked. "I'd never even heard half of what you're telling me. I only read what made the front page of the newspapers: that he'd been nabbed stealing secrets and sent to prison. All of this about The Hole and his murders is new to me."

"That's because you weren't the one assigned to drop him into his victim's houses. And you weren't the one who had to bring him out again, right out of the room with the cooked bodies, and then see what you'd enabled while a bunch of mobsters laughed."

"I can see why how that would have been unpleasant," the prince replied. Vernon didn't like how he was looking at Maia, but he shrugged. He knew that he and Maia were headed—sooner or later—for a violent breakup. They were both too damaged, and damaged along fracture lines that they were both likely to trigger, to stay together. It was just a question of time. Maybe an amicable break in which she was distracted by another guy was the only way for them to remain cordial—

albeit not friends. They weren't even friends now that they were lovers.

"Unpleasant?" Maia said. "If I wasn't a teleporter, if he didn't know that I'd just disappear the second he tried something . . . He seemed the kind of guy who would try to force himself on a woman, just to prove he had the power in the relationship. Or maybe he didn't do it because he knew I'd abandon him on the next teleport. Either way, I was always terrified of what the son of a bitch would try."

"Leave that to me. We can control him," Rod said.

"You try, and I'll teleport the hell out of your life. I'll go so far off the grid that your agents will have to use fucking smoke signals to tell you where I am. *Capisce?*"

"Yes. But at the same time, no." The Pooh Bear stared at them. "We need this guy. And if we don't get him, we could try your method with the ground penetrating radar, but we'd spend weeks going over the ground—weeks we probably won't have, because once the Americans realize what we did, they'll shoot the bird down." Rod paused. "Before you decide, I need you to know something: the Faction has started wider testing of that machine I showed you earlier. In India. They plan to kill a thousand BENT this week, to see how their machine works on multiple targets at once." The bear looked out at them with a completely serious expression. They're moving from testing to production. And we're sitting here sunbathing." He stared straight at Maia. "That had better be some really, really distant part of the Sahara Desert you're thinking of hiding in, because these people are serious, and yours is a particularly easy bend to subvert in a lethal way."

"Fuck," Maia said, letting out an explosive breath.

Chapter 10

Lars wiped the sweat from his eyes and adjusted his hat. He would have been more comfortable with one of the classic pith helmets that the British used to wear, but he'd been warned that a man with his pale skin color wearing one of those in India was likely to be looked at askance.

The man who'd warned him was an upper-class millionaire with a penchant for understatement, so Lars interpreted that to mean that he'd be torn to pieces by a howling mob. The upside was that he'd substituted that perfect piece of headwear for a thoroughly unsatisfying baseball cap, which not only became saturated with sweat almost immediately, but also failed to cover the back of his neck, which meant he was getting sunburned despite the 50-SPF cream he'd slathered all over himself.

"That's the village. Over there." His driver was part of the Faction, an elderly man whose only son had been murdered by a Flash—a man who could move quicker than normal people—who'd wanted to take his wallet. And though the old man was undoubtedly loyal, he hadn't been briefed on what was about to happen, or even warned that something might be about to happen.

The village in question was either completely BENT, or it was something even more dangerous: a different kind of mutation that threatened human ascendancy on Earth.

It was Lars's job to figure out which one, and to deal with it. Apparently, none of the teams with bulky BENT-detection units could be spared from the job of seeking out BENT individuals for use as test subjects.

"Stop the car here, just put it between those two trees," he said.

"Yes, sir."

The air felt thick enough to swim through. Lars had thought that leaving the stuffy, non-air-conditioned car would relieve that, but evidently, the hot wind coming through the windows had actually been a cooling agent. "Ugh. How can people stand to live here?"

He walked through a stand of reeds that grew along the road and studied the village from the cover they provided.

It was a shithole. Small huts constructed from wood, corrugated steel, and even recycled roadside advertising signs lined a tiny dirt path that served as the main street. He knew the villagers were descended from Untouchables—the lowest cast in the now-illegal social system of India's past—but he'd expected more from them.

The people were poor. They were dirty, dressed in grubby rags, and they walked barefoot through the dirt.

But, to a man, woman, and child, they looked well-fed and healthy. Their steps bounced with energy, and their midriffs showed evidence of an excess of calories.

They weren't fat—not yet—but they were moving in that direction, despite certainly not having enough money to spend on food.

Their bend—one inherited by every person in this tiny collection of houses, thirty people in all, and by several thousand others in similar places— was that they could digest the cellulose in plant cells, and extract the nutrients therein. So, if they were ever feeling peckish, they could simply grab a handful of leaves and munch away. Or grass. Or even hay. It would feed them.

Most people had shrugged it off as just another bend, and an unspectacular one at that, but science had never had a close look. Lars wasn't exactly a scientist, but he had a good way to test for it.

His phone buzzed, and he moved back into the reeds to take the call.

"Yeah?" he said.

"Lars," the voice on the other side said. "This is Ove."

"It's good to hear from you. Any activity?"

"None. The coast has been clear in every case. None of the expected activity materialized."

Lars nodded. "Stay vigilant. They might know we know, so they've just set the schedule back." He disconnected the call.

So . . . none of the members of the Committee had been targeted by assassins. No sign of suspicious activity spotted. What did it mean?

It probably meant they had a mole in the organization, and that their preparations to catch whoever was sent in to murder their top people— no matter what their bend might be—had been leaked to the enemy.

It didn't really matter, since a lack of attack was just as good as a failed or thwarted attack as far as the safety of the Committee was concerned, but they'd need to figure out where the information was getting out.

But even more than that, he wanted to understand how the people who'd fed him the tip about the assassination attempts had gotten his number and history. And it would be nice to know whether the murder plot was real or just a ploy to make them commit resources the Norwegian Faction couldn't really afford to spend.

The real mystery, of course, was why they'd come to him instead of communicating with someone behind a desk. It made no sense.

Lars called back to the driver. "Bring my briefcase, please. It's quite heavy, so don't hurt yourself." Though he would have preferred to avoid having the man carry the case around, the old fool would likely have been offended if he'd decided to carry it himself. Important people in India didn't carry their own stuff.

According to headquarters, the current version of the apparatus in the briefcase was quite a lot more powerful, as well as being a little lighter, than the brick he'd lugged around Los Angeles. At this stage, the technology seemed to be getting better week by week.

Power, in this case, meant range. And when one had several targets in sight that essentially had the same bend, range was very useful. He could set the device to redirect the bend and take out several dozen birds with one stone.

Operating the device was child's play. One didn't even, really, need to know what the bend did in detail. The device would allow you to overpower the bend—as he'd done to that freak who thought he was a cloud—or redirect it. Intensify it or turn it off, partially or completely. One of those commands, or a combination of them, would prove lethal in almost every case.

And for those cases where it proved insufficient . . . a bullet to the forehead would work equally well.

This particular case called for simple redirection. So, they had a bend that helped them digest cellulose? Fine. Just redirect it to digest the stomach lining and then, once out of the stomach, the rest of the body.

It wasn't elegant, but it should work.

Impatient with the heat and humidity, he decided to forgo his usual penchant for going slowly to see how the effect developed. He wanted to melt them down and get back to a place with air conditioning. He redirected the bend at the highest strength and waited.

A woman carrying a toddler walked across the street, just a few dozen yards distant. She was absolutely in range, and she should already be feeling the effects of the huge surge of BENT activity.

If she'd been affected by the machine—if, in fact, she'd actually been BENT—then she should be writhing on the floor, her chubby son wailing beside her.

But she walked calmly on until she reached a door, which she opened and ducked inside.

Lars sighed and turned to his driver. "Thank you. I've seen everything I need to see," he told the man. "Take me back to Hyderabad."

A driver somewhere else would have been surprised. In some places, the man would likely have asked what Lars was doing. Or at least his face would have registered an emotion: annoyance at having been dragged out into the middle of nowhere, something. But the man before him simply nodded and carried the briefcase—which he'd held in his hand the entire time—to the car.

Then he started the motor and drove.

One could get used to India, Lars observed.

Standing waist-deep in a pool at a rooftop terrace bar, a private residence high above Hyderabad, one of a line of identical buildings superimposed over the skyline, Lars sipped a gin and tonic, satellite phone pressed to his ear.

He waited while several layers of encryption were validated and checked. Finally, a voice came onto the line. He wondered who it was, and whether the voice was real or disguised. All he had was a name that had to be a cover identity: Isis.

Of course, the person on the other side referred to him as Lars, so he couldn't complain.

The major difference, he suspected, was that she knew precisely who he really was, while he genuinely had no clue.

"Lars," the mellifluous tones said. "You have news?"

"I have news," he replied. "They aren't BENT."

"You're sure?"

"Unless the unit is malfunctioning, yes."

"That is unlikely. We will need to send a second excursion in to deal with these people."

The owner of the voice didn't elaborate, but Lars suspected the next team would go in at night armed with large drums of poison for a considerable number of village wells. And as the man on the ground . . .

"Would you like me to begin coordinating the movements?" he said.

A long silence ensued. "No. This will require two steps. In the first, we'll need to send people down to double-check your findings. They'll discard the possibility that your unit was malfunctioning, and verify that the genetic and radiation markers aren't BENT-positive. Once that's done, we'll make our move on them. That will take some time, and the project you're currently on is moving a little too quickly for us to be able to pull you off."

"Understood." He breathed a sigh of relief. The Indian Mutants, as they were known on the few occasion when anyone bothered to write about the tiny villages lost in the subcontinent's countryside, were a classical target for Human Rights groups. As such, when they were attacked, the police forces of every nation in the world would come after the suspects with every resource they had.

Whoever poisoned those wells, and the people who handled them, would fall. And Lars had always prided himself on not being one of the losers who took the rap for terrorist activities.

The voice went on. "Stay where you are. You will receive further instructions within the next three hours. Discard your current identity papers. You will be issued new ones at the airport."

The line went dead.

Lars grinned. Often, his handlers would already have his next assignment ready to go. Three hours actually meant he had a little time to enjoy himself. He approached the man behind the bar.

"Earlier, you offered entertainment. I assumed you meant women," Lars said.

The barman gave him a half-smile. "Women, men, something in between. The master is not judgmental, and he has everything his guests might want directly to hand. The only thing he will not supply are entertainers with bends."

Lars kept his features placid. He would have bet his life savings, a considerable fortune, that his host—a well-known Bollywood studio owner— would supply whatever bend anyone desired if the business he was conducting required it, but he wasn't stupid enough to offer them to the representative of the Norwegian Faction. "Women are fine," Lars replied. "I find that I have a few hours on my hand and no pressing business to spend it on."

"How very fortunate, sir," the barman replied. "The doors along the corridor on the far side of the pool open to the private rooms. What is your preference? Is there any ethnicity or hair color you prefer?"

"Surprise me," Lars replied. "The only thing I really need is that she knows how to give a killer massage."

"Of course, sir." The man almost looked affronted. "Our staff consists solely of the most highly-trained professionals." He smiled. "I assure you that you will be satisfied."

"Thank you."

Chapter 11

The forest ended at the edge of the cliff, as if a giant had decided to hack a cross section of the mountain away with an axe. One minute, the team was walking between the thickly-packed trees, and the next, they were looking out over a colossal hole in the ground.

"That," the mercenary colonel in charge of the soldiers in the group informed them, "is the largest strip mine in the world. Or at least it was until the fall of the Soviet Union. It is probably responsible for poisoning more rivers than anything else ever invented." He shrugged. "Of course, now it's the world's crappiest prison, and the place they'll lock us if we manage to screw this mission up."

Vernon peered down into the mine. The hole looked like a strip mine, the deserted remains of capitalist—or in this case communist—consumption. He vaguely wondered what commodity was pulled out of this scar in the Earth's skin, but didn't care enough to ask.

The colonel checked his watch and looked back at them. "The initial strike team is in position. We have thirty minutes to get a few hundred meters further along this cliff. Move it."

Vernon wondered where Rod had gotten the colonel. The man was six feet five and built like an MMA star, clean-shaven, blond-haired, and blue-eyed. The eyes never showed any emotion whatsoever. If someone had built up a composite image of a guy who would be wanted across the developing war for a litany of war crimes, his would be the picture they came up with. He spoke English with an accent, but one that was hard to pin down. Vernon guessed he might be South African . . . albeit too young to have been active in the military before Apartheid fell apart.

They retreated a little further into the trees and began to hike at a good clip, encumbered by the ever-present trunks. The entire trip had been a slow, grueling affair. They'd teleported to a flyspeck town in Siberia before boarding six trucks and driving at ridiculously slow speeds toward the facility.

Rod, who'd only beamed his avatar into the first town before going dark, had explained that anything—transmissions, teleports, high-speed bend incursions—that came within fifty kilometers of The Hole would be detected, analyzed, and hit by the most appropriate attack team.

Ironically, this meant that the best way to get in there without a fight against overwhelming odds was to walk.

So, they walked for a day and a night to reach their current position. They didn't walk too quickly, and they stopped for rest periods, but it had been quite the hike all the same.

And now came the hard part.

"Stop," the colonel said, holding up a hand. "We're here."

A ramp had been built into the rock, but more importantly, the entrance to The Hole could be seen in the center of the space below them, just five hundred meters from their position. Concrete turrets surrounded the entrance, and six barracks buildings lay end to end.

Minutes later, the colonel raised his watch again. "Ten, nine, eight," the man said.

When he reached zero, a bright light flashed from the entrance. Moments later, the ground shook and the noise hit.

"Amen," said the soldiers around them when the blast died down.

Vernon looked Maia's way, to see what the joke was. She rolled her eyes. "You didn't pay attention during the briefing, did you?"

"Of course I did. I know exactly what I'm supposed to do, and when I'm supposed to do it."

"But you weren't listening about the kinetic weapons?" Maia asked.

"Of course. They drop from satellites, don't they? Metal bars or something."

"Or something, yeah," Maia said. "Those weapons have a nickname. The soldiers call them 'Rods from God,' which is why they say 'amen' after a strike."

Now it was Vernon's turn to roll his eyes. "Oh, come on," he groaned.

"Not my fault," Maia said.

"Go, go, go!" the colonel shouted. He sprinted toward the ramp, which now looked like it led into a bowl filled with clouds, due to the dust raised by the strike. Gunfire emerged from within.

The colonel gave them a running report. "Those are FALs, which means that's our people doing the firing. The guards all use AKs."

Twenty soldiers accompanied the colonel, who'd been tasked with ensuring that the BENT members of the team got in safely. That was a tall order, as the facility had been specifically designed to deal with any kind of bend that might get thrown their way. It was well-equipped both to keep the inmates contained and to keep their friends from coming after them.

Ironically, the one thing the facility had never been designed for was a low-tech armed incursion by guys with guns.

Of course, if those guys with guns could even the odds out a bit by hijacking military satellites from a major nation-state and using high-precision kinetic weapons that couldn't be detected, that helped, too. A prison out in the middle of nowhere wouldn't expect to be hit by weapons owned only by a handful of governments. Not in peacetime. Or at any time, really.

But, thanks to Rod's incredible hacking prowess, that was what had just happened.

The fight inside the dust cloud was getting closer.

"Take cover behind that pile of rubble," the colonel told the BENTs, before rushing blindly into the fray.

Trying to keep his head down, Vernon explored the rubble. It turned out to be the upturned lip of a crater that, as far as he could tell, occupied the spot where one of the barracks had been earlier.

At least the hundred guards inside wouldn't have felt a thing; they'd have been vaporized instantly. As the dust began to clear, Vernon realized that the same could be said for the men in the other barracks and in the guard posts. Wooden buildings or concrete bunkers, the result was the same: they'd been replaced with deep holes in the rocky ground.

Three minutes later, the colonel returned. "We're in," he said. "Move."

Vernon marveled at the accuracy of the weapons. They were incredibly destructive, of course, but they destroyed what they were aimed at and nothing else. The only structure remaining, untouched among piles of rubble, was the entrance to the prison.

A long concrete ramp emerged from the ground to become the roof of a wide tunnel. The entrance to the tunnel stood before them, and it could have served as the entrance to any office building in any financial center in the world.

This one would have been a financial center after being bombed by terrorists, however; bullet holes in the concrete and shattered glass everywhere, as well as a couple of dead guards, provided evidence of things having gone sideways—but the bones were still there. Steel pillars had supported the plate glass windows, Bauhaus chairs stood around little center tables, and the logo of some kind of Russian corrective organization could be seen through the dust on the marble floor. The lighting was smooth and professional.

A blonde receptionist in a corporate-looking blue suit sat behind a long black desk. A coin-sized hole in her forehead showed the place where one of the colonel's men had plugged her. The door to the actual jail beyond was separated from the reception room by two turnstiles.

Ten steps beyond the turnstiles, an armored steel curtain had been blown open by charges. Two of the colonel's men were packing away a field detonator.

The tunnel beyond was pitch black, cut only by the flashlights held by the troops. The sound of gunfire emerged from it.

"Okay, little boys and girls," the colonel said. "The cakewalk is over. Now, you need to be on guard, because shit is going to get real. And remember that this place is designed to keep people like you from overpowering the guards. So, expect to be hit with poison gas, high-frequency sounds that will keep you from concentrating, low frequency sounds meant to keep your bodies vibrating and stop you from bending stuff, pressure waves, light pulsations, radiation, and anything else they've thought up to keep the BENT from wrecking the guards." He paused. "Your best bet would be to let my people take care of the defense apparatus before you advance too far." He shrugged. "My job is to keep you guys alive, because the boss thinks we'll need you to break down the final defenses. Fair enough. No one knows what's in there. But the truth is that my people will be busy, so you need to be careful. The only one of you I'm going to actually be watching is the teleport; we need her to get us home."

Having told them how much he loved them, the colonel walked into the tunnel, keeping to the walls.

The group of BENT followed his example. Sarena had gone completely transparent, and her clothing began to drop to the floor. The royals had clasped one another's hands.

"Can you hear that?" Maia asked.

"What?"

"That sound. High-pitched. Like *piiiii*," she made a noise like the beep from a watch alarm.

Vernon listened. Their footsteps echoed in the darkness. Water dripped. "I . . . think so. Barely."

"It's going around and around in my head. If this goes on, I won't be able to port," Maia said.

"Really?"

"Yeah, really. So, we'd better find the origin and kill it, or we're going to need to get back outside before we jump."

Vernon thought about what she was telling him. He'd never bothered thinking about how other bends worked. He didn't even think about his own. It just functioned. His skin did what he needed it to do, and he was safe. But others needed to think, to direct their bends . . . and a defense like this one that could get in your head would be brilliant against a teleport, for example, if it stopped her from thinking.

He wondered what other surprises lay in store.

Instead of corkscrewing around itself, which was a good way to minimize the footprint of any long subterranean tunnel structure, the passage—wide and tall enough to drive a couple of cement trucks through side by side—drilled straight forward. Of course, Siberia was, for all intents and purposes, infinite, so the people who'd built the place probably hadn't worried about the size of the installation.

Or maybe they were concerned about getting hit from above. The logical way to destroy a compound like this one would have been to nuke it and attempt to bury it under the intervening rock. But if the important part wasn't directly below the entrance . . . then nuking it would require knowing exact coordinates of the prison structure. You couldn't destroy something you couldn't find.

Vernon suspected that none of the above-ground guards knew exactly where the tunnel went.

And keeping the below-ground team in the dark should pose little problem.

His suspicions were confirmed when the tunnel suddenly turned ninety degrees and continued merrily on its way, no end in sight. It would be nearly impossible for anyone to pinpoint precisely where they were by dead reckoning alone.

Five of the colonel's men waited at a small widening of the tunnel, which was full of golf carts and sweeping machines. Two more dead guards lay on the floor, riddled with bullets.

"We thought you might appreciate a ride, sir," the nearest said with a salute. "The forward team are all mounted up."

"I hope those things don't have tracking chips," the colonel said dourly. Then he shrugged. "Well, if they do, it's Heine's problem now. How many of these carts did he take?"

"About a dozen," the soldier replied.

"Why in the world do they have so many?"

"I don't know, sir."

"All right"—the colonel turned back to the team of BENT—"Hop on. Four to a cart. Anyone who isn't a total moron at the wheel is invited to drive."

They whirred into the tunnel and drove for what seemed like a really long time. Finally, gunfire and explosions could be heard again, which meant they were at least getting close to something interesting.

And then a hand closed around his head and squeezed.

Vernon blacked out.

Chapter 12

Vernon opened his eyes.

"Dammit, shine that somewhere else," he snarled. "What are you trying to do, blind me?"

Maia, who'd been the one holding his head and shining a flashlight in his eyes pulled away. "He's fine. That crabbiness is just his way of saying how much we mean to him."

She helped him to his feet, and he felt woozy for a moment. "What the hell was that?" he asked when the dizziness passed.

"Pressure wave."

"Damn," he said. Vernon didn't bother to think about most things that could hurt him. His skin could protect him against a lot of stuff. He even suspected that it had some way to block a certain amount of radiation simply by playing with air molecules near his skin. But pressure, which went straight into his unprotected earholes, was a different story. It was one of his weak points. "Did it take us down?"

"Just you. The rest of us barely felt it."

"Fuck," Vernon said. "This could really cramp my style." Then he looked around the corridor. "Who were you talking to, just then?"

"Me," Sarena's voice came out of the darkness in the direction of the cart the rest of the crew had left them. "They needed the space on the carts, and I didn't want to sit on a soldier's lap without clothes on. If it makes you feel better, I did feel the wave. It was like being on a plane when they pressurize the cabin."

"It was a lot worse than that," Vernon said.

"It's a question of what each of us feels. I hear the pinging as if I was inside a bell. You can barely hear it. Each of us is sensitive to different things. That's how they control the dangerous BENT in this facility."

They mounted the golf cart and pointed its nose toward the commotion up ahead. The firefight didn't seem to have died down. If anything, it had gotten worse.

"Over there," Sarena said.

"How can you see with transparent eyes?" Maia said. "Shouldn't the light pass straight through them?"

"I've never thought about that," Sarena replied. "I guess it comes with the whole turning invisible thing."

Maia chuckled. "You should get together to compare notes with Vernon. Neither of you has a clue as to what you're doing. But seriously, I'm so glad I'm not a physicist right now. Do you imagine what it must be like trying to make science work with all the bends out there? And as soon as you explain one, another inexplicable piece of crap crops up?"

"Maybe they're the ones who are bankrolling the Norwegian Faction. Disgruntled men in lab coats," Vernon replied.

"I can see the main room now. We're getting close," Maia said.

Vernon squinted. His vision was still blurry from the shock wave, but there was definitely a patch of light somewhere up ahead. And the sounds of combat were getting closer. He just hoped those waves wouldn't affect his capacity to defend himself.

Maia, who was driving, slowed to a crawl as they approached a spot where the tunnel widened in every direction to become a cavernous room draped in shadow—with occasional spots of light.

The brightest illuminated area was the space around one of the carts, which was in flames. Four of the colonel's men lay dead around it.

"They've got missile launchers," Maia whispered.

"Who?" Vernon hissed back.

"The guards. Look."

As his eyes got used to the gloom and some of the fuzziness disappeared, Vernon studied the place they'd reached. They were at the bottom of a cylindrical chamber, which towered at least ten stories above them—probably more, but the far reaches were lost in the gloom. Balconies ran across each level and, on those balconies, Vernon could see dark figures scurrying. Guards? The colonel's men? It was impossible to tell which were which, but the fact that they were mixed up was evidenced by the dynamics. Groups would open fire at what seemed like random intervals at each other. When one group was down, the other would continue to advance in a mission and direction known only to themselves.

"Where are the royals?" Maia said.

Transparent or not, Sarena apparently had incredible eyes, because she responded long before

Vernon even had a chance to scan the nearest balconies. "Over there."

"Are you pointing? Because we can't see you," Vernon said.

"Second level, beside the fire."

"Yeah, I see them now."

Once he knew where they were, the two were easy to spot. Unlike the huddled men looking for any cover they could find on the exposed balconies, the prince and princess stood tall, hand in hand, advancing at the head of a group of soldiers and offering their chests to the oncoming bullets. On occasion, one of the guards would get too close and immediately arc across the open space to land with a sickening crunch on the concrete below, impelled by the super strength of one of the siblings.

"They should stay back," Maia said, shaking her head. "The prince is the only one who knows where Eyespy is. The cell number, I mean."

"Where Rod thinks Eyespy is," Vernon said. "He didn't sound too confident. Also, I want to know why he didn't tell all of us."

"I think he has a long history with the prince. He trusts the man."

Vernon snorted. "That won't do us much good if he gets himself killed."

A soldier discharged a magazine into the prince's chest. The noble didn't even flinch, and dispatched the man with a ballet kick that took his head off. The guard's dead body stood for a moment as if unsure how to react to that, then collapsed in a heap.

"I don't think we need to worry about that," Maia replied. "We should get up there."

"What for?" Vernon asked. "They look like they can take care of things perfectly well without us."

"Yeah. Except that door over there is the entrance to the control room. That's where all the really ugly stuff like gas saturation and that kind of thing is going to be concentrated. Not even Rod knows what kind of nasties are back there, so we need to get over there. Particularly you and Sarena. Ideally, we'd need to get in without tripping any optic sensors. That's Sarena's role." She shrugged. "But if we don't, that's where you come in. You really weren't listening to the briefing, were you?"

"I just figured that, with a hundred guys with machine guns on our side, we'd be okay. Can you jump us up there?"

"Not until someone finds the thing generating the noise."

"Crap, is it really that bad?" Vernon replied. "I can hardly hear it."

"It's not loud, as much as . . . I dunno, deep, I guess. It's like something I can feel inside my head, and it makes it impossible for me to put my mind in the right place to teleport," Maia replied.

Normally, Vernon would have grunted and shrugged at people who had to concentrate so hard on something that should come naturally, but he realized that unless they found the source of the noise, they would be stuck there. "Can you tell me where it's coming from?"

Maia stood still for a second. "Precisely? No. But I feel it coming from over there, somewhere." She pointed toward a wall opposite the fighting, where only a pair of people in guard uniforms huddled. They didn't appear to be armed, and looked more scared than belligerent, although they might have been faking it. At that distance, it was kind of hard to see if they had holsters or not.

"Okay. Let's go take it out."

"We need to go with the royals," Maia insisted.

"It will take me all day to fight my way through those guys with guns. And you and Sarena will end up getting shot, even if they can't see her. There's a lot of hot lead flying around over there. It's much faster to teleport. Come on."

He didn't wait for her to answer. Someone needed to take out the source of those vibrations, and it might as well be him. Maia waited half a beat, but she followed, and Vernon assumed Sarena was coming, too.

Sprinting straight across the open space would have drawn fire from both sides, so they hugged the far wall, a longer but considerably safer route. In fact, Vernon was reasonably confident that they hadn't even been fired on once, and that the scattered bullets falling around them were due more to the sheer volume of the fight at the other side of the enormous room than anything to do with them.

They reached a staircase and headed up.

Vernon stopped at the first floor. He turned to Maia. "Is it getting stronger?"

Maia nodded, apparently too affected by the vibration to do much more than that. She pointed up and to the left. One more floor, apparently.

Now Vernon could feel it, too. A high-pitched whine that he felt in his teeth more than with his ears. A human dog whistle, one that made being in its vicinity uncomfortable.

Maia's hand landed on Vernon's shoulder. He looked back, and she shook her head. Her face had—even in the orangish lights of the stairs—taken on a greenish tinge.

Vernon understood. "Stay here," he said. Then, without checking whether Sarena was with him—the ghost wouldn't be much use against physical resistance—he sprinted up the steps, taking them two by two. On the next level, the sensation was almost overwhelming, a sense of pins and needles all over Vernon's body.

"Dammit," he said, but his tongue was too fuzzy to talk. The word emerged as 'Duuut.'

A guard—he couldn't have been more than eighteen or nineteen, some wet-behind-the-ears new recruit—stood before him, a pistol in a shaking hand.

But even with the shakes, he couldn't miss from that range, and as the gun went off, Vernon grimaced. Though the bullet didn't penetrate his skin, getting hit at really close range was never fun. That one would leave a bruise.

Vernon took a step forward and grabbed the gun, his anger at allowing himself to be surprised making him rash. It melted and bubbled before dribbling to the floor. Then he grabbed the collar of the boy's uniform.

But his bend didn't do anything. Deep down, Vernon must have known that this kid was out of the fight. He could be allowed to live.

Vernon sighed and let him go. The boy ran off along the balcony, leaving a puddle of wetness behind.

Years from now, Vernon knew, that boy would likely drink himself to death, living and reliving the day when he pissed himself in fear and ran away from a battle.

But only if he survived.

Forcing himself to advance into the screeching beep, Vernon tried to locate the source of the offending vibrations. A large conical shape that looked like a piece of wall stood where the emissions appeared to be generated.

He rapped his knuckles against it and confirmed that it was just a concrete protuberance. That meant the generator must be on the other side.

Which sucked, because it always took a while to melt concrete.

Suddenly, he had an idea. If the concrete shell surrounded whatever apparatus was in there making his teeth grind together, then the cables that powered it would come from the back. If he could get to them . . .

Vernon put his hands where the regular wall met the concrete cone and began melting it away. Fortunately, the protection—concrete reinforced by metal mesh—was only five centimeters thick at this point, and he was able to cut through in under a minute. As soon as he had an opening wide enough, he shone his light through, illuminating the interior of the cone.

There. One cable. He couldn't quite reach it, but that wasn't a problem. He pulled the handgun he'd been assigned out of his holster, aimed at a connector that looked important, and fired.

Nothing happened, so he fired again.

And suddenly, it was as if the weight of the world had come off his shoulders. He hadn't realized just how much the vibration had hurt until it was gone. Then it was like seeing the sun after a year of rain. It was like living under a huge weight to find it suddenly gone.

He turned back to see Maia running up the stairs in tears. But she was laughing, and she threw her arms around him. Another—unseen—pair of arms also encircled him, and Vernon realized Sarena had been with them all along.

"Can we jump now?" he asked.

"Wherever you want," Maia replied. Then she planted a kiss full on his lips.

"How about over there, all the way across this room, about ten yards behind the royals on that balcony on the second level? I think I see some doorways where we can take cover."

"I can do that," Maia said, and suddenly, they were there.

Vernon quickly shoved Maia and Sarena into the shadow of a door. From inside, a voice could be heard demanding to know what the fuck was going on. Maia told the guy to shut up.

Up ahead, the prince and princess were wrecking any guards they could lay their hands on and, by dint of throwing and kicking all kinds of debris at them, many they couldn't physically reach.

Vernon strode out to join them, drawing quite a lot of fire, which he ignored.

Just as he was about to pull even with the two magnificent fighters, one of the guards screamed something in Russian and threw a canister at them. It landed about two yards short of their position and, before Vernon could react, it exploded.

Instinctively, he closed his mouth and lowered his goggles.

But the damage had been done. A dense cloud of blue gas enveloped both Vernon and the royals.

The princess gasped, choked, and released the prince's hand.

Unaffected by whatever the gas was—he assumed it was something you had to breathe in order to be hurt—Vernon took two steps, grabbed the princess's hand, and was about to get it into contact with her brother's, when the prince's head, the head that contained the location of Eyespy's cell, exploded in a shower of gore, impacted by a round from a guard's rifle.

Chapter 13

"No!" screamed the princess.

Vernon shielded her with his body and dragged her to where Maia waited. The gas must have lost much of its potency with distance, because, other than covering her face with her shirt, Maia didn't seem to be having too much difficulty with it.

He pushed the screaming, struggling princess into Maia's arms. "Get her out of here and come back when I finish with those assholes over there."

Maia nodded, and both she and the princess blinked out of existence.

The colonel's troops surged past. Maybe a dozen of them.

There seemed to be much fewer troops on their side than they'd started off with. This dozen was the largest remaining group, and the colonel himself was nowhere to be seen.

As Vernon watched, two of the soldiers got mowed down. "Get behind cover," he shouted. "Let me through."

They obeyed, and Vernon strode, powered by a fury he hadn't felt in a long time, toward the mass of guards. Their numbers appeared to be pretty thin as well, but five were guarding a door. That must have been the royals' objective, so that was the door Vernon was going to open.

The guards' position was quite good; they had dragged a couple of metal lockers out onto the balcony and were huddled behind them, safe from gunfire.

Unfortunately for them, Vernon had no intention of using his gun.

They sprayed a cloud of bullets in his direction, but he simply closed his eyes and advanced, opening his eyes only occasionally to see where he was going—a bullet in the eyeball would have ruined his whole day.

When he got to the first locker, a man attempted to break Vernon's nose with the butt of a rifle.

The rifle melted, and Vernon put his hands on the man's cheeks. He didn't even press hard, but smoke immediately began to rise from his opponent's face, and the man screamed in terror before pulling away and running off, leaving some kind of goop on Vernon's palms.

He went through them in a daze, too angry to care that one of the guards was a pretty young woman. He melted her face off just like the last one. He didn't care that another guard was too young to die. They all died or ran off disfigured before Vernon stood in front of the door.

Then, he melted that out of the way as well, bubbling the thick armor to vapor and regretting only that he couldn't tear it from its hinges and throw it all the way across the enormous room to embed itself in the concrete of the far wall. Super strength might not be as versatile as his own bend, but it was definitely a great way to vent.

The next room looked like mission control in Houston. Rows of desks with built-in computer consoles illuminated the space. He steeled himself to withstand poison gas, pressure waves, deadly radiation, unbearable ultrasonics.

None of it came, and the reason was quickly apparent. The room was full of people. Some seated, a few huddled against the furthest wall.

All of them terrified.

He didn't care. Here were the people, the victims, who would help him work through his anger. There were about fifteen of them. Not enough to calm him down, perhaps, but it would be a start.

A hand on his shoulder stopped him. "Don't," Maia said.

He turned to look at her.

"I'm going to kill them all," he said.

"We need them. If you kill these people, the prince will have died for nothing."

"I don't care about the fucking prince," he replied. "But did you see how the princess reacted? She's going to be a wreck for a long time."

"You really were falling in love with her?"

"I . . ." Vernon stopped. "I don't know. I just saw her tearing at her hair, and something clicked. But I don't think it's love. It's more that I realized what the people we're trying to stop are doing, and what this whole facility is about. Both are about keeping the BENT in their place. And killing the prince was just a part of that. The princess knew, and I think her grief is also larger than the death of her brother."

"We should probably discuss this later," Maia said.

Everyone in the room was staring at them like they were demons just out of hell about to tear them apart.

"I'm okay, now," Vernon said. He walked into the room. The people who'd been working there pressed as far back as they could go, as if his mere presence could somehow harm them. He supposed that might be true of some of the people locked in this facility; you had to be a serious threat to public safety to be thrown in The Hole. He scanned their faces. Every eye followed his movements. Finally, his gaze halted on one man, a little older than the rest, his clothing well-aligned, his hair well-cut. But what caught Vernon's eye was the watch. It looked expensive. "All right," he said. "I won't kill you all. But you have to help me. Do you speak English?"

The man responded something in Russian.

Vernon took three steps toward him and placed the bare skin of his hand against the top of the man's head. He didn't pull it away until a few seconds later, when half of the head had melted away with the smell of frying bacon.

"Let's try that again," he said to the room. "I know you speak English. Now, I want to know which one of you will help me. If everyone doesn't volunteer within the next five seconds, I'll just kill you. If you do, I promise you I won't kill any of the people in this room. How's that?"

A woman took a trembling step forward. "I speak English," she said.

"See? It isn't that hard. I need to find a prisoner. His name is Eyespy."

The woman took three rapid steps backward and put her hands up.

"What?" Vernon asked.

"We . . . we can't," the woman stammered.

"You don't want to fuck with me. Not today," Vernon replied.

"I didn't say we won't. We can't. It's not possible for any of us."

"Why the fuck not? You can open the cell doors, right?"

"Yes, yes," the woman said. "But I can't get this Eyespy out."

"Why?" Even Vernon could hear the ice in his voice. The woman shrank back further.

"Because none of us know the identity of the prisoners. Not here in the control room, not the guards. Some supervisors know which prisoners have dangerous bends, and they control the deployment of suppression equipment, but we don't. Not in here. I have never even seen one of the prisoners. Our doors are always closed when one of them is removed from his cell."

"Fuck. And where can I find a supervisor?" Vernon asked.

The woman shrugged. "I don't know. All we do here is keep watch on the prisoners' vital signs and monitor whether they're building up to some kind of aggressive manifestation. And we open the doors when a guard asks us to."

Vernon turned to Maia. "Bring me the colonel."

Maia blinked out of existence. Moments later, she reappeared with the colonel in tow.

"We need to grab a supervisor alive," Vernon told him.

"You should have said so earlier," the colonel replied. "I don't think there are any left. A couple of guards we haven't shot down. Maybe some snipers on the top level, but the officers? We took them down first thing. And I'm glad we did, too. I don't think I have more than ten men still standing. I'll need to spend my entire fee from this job just rebuilding my unit."

"Fuck," Vernon spat.

"There's another thing," the colonel said.

"What?"

"Reinforcements. Not ours, theirs. They're at the top of the tunnel. The two men I left as lookouts just arrived to inform me of that. We booby-trapped the tunnel . . . but that will only slow them for a few minutes. They'll be on top of us in half an hour."

"How the hell am I supposed to figure out which cell has Eyespy in it?" Vernon said. "I can't see him."

"I'd suggest you do it quickly," the colonel replied. "Because we need to get the hell out of here."

"Double fuck," Vernon said.

Maia stepped between them. "Men," she said with a sigh. "Too dumb to see what's in front of their eyes. We can solve both problems at once."

"How?" Vernon asked.

"Open all the doors. Every cell. Point the inmates at the bad guys and grab Eyespy on the way out. I can recognize him."

"No!" The words came from the woman who'd been talking to them. The guard lady who spoke English. "You can't do that."

"And who is going to stop us?" Vernon asked calmly.

"Those prisoners are murderers. Terrorists. Rapists. Scum," the woman said.

He looked around the room. "If every cell isn't open by the time I count to three, everyone in this room will die."

"We'll die anyway. Those people—"

"*Might* kill you," Vernon broke in. "I *will* kill you. There's a slight chance for you if you do what I say." He took a deep breath. "One . . . Two . . ."

Every person in the room began manipulating control boards, except for the woman who'd spoken earlier. She just stood there, pale, aghast, trembling. "No, no, no," she whispered.

Vernon looked away. Despite his threats, he wouldn't kill the woman. Somehow, he could tell that she wasn't afraid for herself. She was afraid of what the prisoners would do.

He tried not to think about that. Maybe he would just avoid watching the news for a few days. What he didn't know wouldn't hurt him, right?

He stepped to the door of the command chamber and watched the prisoners emerge from their cells. Some burst out and headed for the exit as quickly as their feet could carry them. Some emerged slowly, blinking and befuddled.

One man laughed and sprayed the chamber with bright beams from his hands, catching one of the fleeing prisoners in the beams and burning him to a crisp.

"That's him," Maia said, pointing to a man who'd walked out calmly and seemed to be surveying the scene. He thought for a moment and then headed toward the stairs that led to the control room.

"Do you think you can bring him here?" Vernon asked.

"I won't give him a choice."

She disappeared and reappeared so quickly that Vernon barely realized she'd gone. Except that she had a man with her.

Or towering over her. He was a gigantic guy with steel-gray buzz-cut hair who blinked for a moment, then turned to look at her.

He smiled grimly. "Maia, what a pleasant surprise. I assume Viktor sent you to get me?"

"Viktor's been dead for two years," Maia said. "Someone cut his throat. The Magadan Chapter has been dissolved. You and I are probably the only ones left. Everyone else is dead. Ugly dead."

Eyespy laughed. "You mean I'm alive because the pigs locked me up?"

"Probably," Maia said.

"How delicious," Eyespy replied. "Then you didn't come get me?"

"She did," Vernon said, interrupting the lovefest. He definitely didn't like how Eyespy was looking at Maia. "We all did. We've come to offer you a job."

"Is it the kind of job one is allowed to decline?" Eyespy asked.

"Not my call to make. Now, come on, we're leaving."

The big man turned back to Maia. "How rude. Breaking into my house and ordering me around. Give me one good reason why I shouldn't give this little rooster brain cancer."

"Because if you do, I'll teleport you to orbit and leave you there."

"Very well," Eyespy sighed. "You always did insist on acting as my conscience."

"Get the colonel," Vernon told Maia. "Round up the troops and get us out of here."

She nodded, and a minute or so later, just as the screams and gunfire were beginning to intensify again, Vernon, Eyespy, Sarena, the colonel, and his seven surviving men winked out of The Hole, leaving the former inmates to work out their frustrations against the men coming through the tunnel, and the people in the control room to fend for themselves.

Vernon thought it would have been fun to film. A lot of people would have paid good money to see that on PPV. Blood always paid.

Especially when most of the people doing the dying would deserve everything they got.

Chapter 14

Lars stared at the news on the screen in Frankfurt airport as he awaited his suitcase. The BENT who'd been locked in The Hole had escaped and gone on a rampage. The image showed the smoking ruins of a little rural town in Siberia, where a man with his arm in a sling wept over the bodies of his wife and children.

"This is why we need to eliminate them," he growled.

As if in response, his phone rang. The smooth, modulated voice he'd spoken to in Hyderabad spoke before he even answered. "There's been a change of plans," it informed him. "So, you have the apparatus with you?"

"Of course. I wouldn't dream of checking it."

"Good. Then head to desk forty-seven. They have your next ticket waiting. But hurry, the gate closes in thirty minutes."

"I was waiting for my suitcase," Lars said.

"Leave it. We'll have someone pick it up, and I'll make certain you have clothes when you arrive."

Lars hesitated. "Where am I going?"

"Yakutsk," the voice replied. "And it's the only flight going out this week."

"Where the hell is that?" Lars asked.

"Siberia," the voice replied.

Lars smiled.

Lars dove clear of the helicopter just as the fireball slammed into its rotor. He rolled and came to a stop behind the car that had come to meet him. Turning back, he saw that the chopper was still mostly intact, and that the pilot and copilot were bailing out. Two security people that had been in the car opened up on a small copse of trees, presumably, the source of the ambush.

But Lars wasn't watching the fight. He was scanning the floor in search of the briefcase with the device. He'd dropped it on his way out of the aircraft.

There. It lay on its side in the grass, half-hidden by one of the helicopter's wheels. He sprinted back to its position just as a second fireball hit the car he'd been huddling behind.

He pulled the case to relative safety behind the helicopter fuselage—it didn't seem like the fireballs were particularly powerful, and it would likely take a few more shots to burn through the chopper.

Unfortunately for him, that bastard of a BENT didn't have a few shots to spare. Now that the case was safe, he would use it.

Lars pulled out his cell phone and activated the device within the briefcase. He set it to its maximum level and set it to direct the bend at its owner. In some cases, that would have been a stupid thing to do, since things like super strength would only help the attacker.

But in the case of a bend that launched fireballs . . .

A shriek sounded from the trees, a thin sound that soon dissolved into nothing.

Lars stood. "Hold your fire," he barked at the security guys. Then he repeated the order in Russian, just in case.

They raised an eyebrow at him, but, to their credit, they lowered their handguns. Professionals who knew what they were doing. Good.

"I've neutralized the threat. Now, let's go see what we're left with," Lars said.

"Yes, sir," the nearest man said.

Lars set the device on the grass, tasked the pilots—who were staring at their aircraft in disbelief—with guarding it, and headed toward the trees. The security guys followed, but he noted that they hadn't holstered their guns.

The little stand of trees stood on a hill beside the little meadow they used to land helicopters on. Lars followed the smell of cooking meat and emerged into a little clearing where a young woman, with charred skin and wearing the molten remains of a prison uniform, keened softly to herself.

He stamped out a little brush fire and knelt beside her. "Does it hurt?" he asked.

She tried to open her eyes, which broke the charred skin above the ridge of her nose and caused her to scream.

"I'll take that as a yes." Lars leaned in and whispered in her ear. "And I'm happy it does. If it's any comfort to you, at least we won't try to save you and put you in a burn ward or anything. You're going to die out here, like the worthless scum you are." Then he stood up and looked down at her. "Hmm. You aren't that badly crisped. Barely enough to kill you, and slowly at that. Not much of a bend. Most of the fireball launchers I know would have burned a mere person to ashes. Not to mention, they would have blown the chopper to bits as well. I hope the rest of the BENT around here are more worthwhile than you, because if not, I'll be really pissed that I came all the way out here to suppress your little prison riot."

He stood up and walked away.

"What should we do with her?" one of the security guys asked.

Lars shrugged. "Shoot her, let her die. Whatever you like. She's very unlikely to annoy anyone ever again. Now, do you think that car will run?" He indicated the vehicle that was still smoking from the fireball attack. "I'm kind of in a hurry."

A house stood at the coordinates they'd sent him. There was absolutely nothing special about the house. Faded white paint covered rough wooden boards, and the windows appeared to have been installed grudgingly, as if someone had measured the need for light as opposed to the need for warmth that would escape out of a window and wondered whether it was worth the sacrifices. Small windows had carried the day.

Snow, a December flurry—unusual only in that it fell on ground that didn't already have a deep snow cover—half-hid the woods behind the house, but hadn't yet managed to cover the body of the man who lay dead in the footpath in front of the door.

The man was dressed in a brown jacket stained with the blood that had spattered everywhere when his head exploded.

Lars, hidden in a stand of trees across the road, could hear pleading from inside, the desperate yells of a woman who knew her nearest neighbor was two miles away. The yells of a woman who knew that if she ran, she would join her husband as a headless corpse.

The BENT who had the woman captive was a Frenchman wanted in almost every country in the world. He was a murderer, as evidenced by the corpse, but that wasn't his main thing. He was a sicko on several levels who got his kicks by forcing people into disgusting activities they would never have performed willingly.

Lars had assumed he was some kind of sexual predator, but, again, that was only a sideline, the tip of the iceberg. This bastard liked watching people do disgusting stuff. He would only force them to have sex with him afterward, after he'd watched them debase themselves. Men, women, children, it all seemed indifferent to him.

And his methods were simple: walk into a room somewhere and explain that anyone who didn't do exactly what they were told would die, with their heads exploded. A couple of examples would suffice to keep everyone else quiet and submissive.

Had he been a writer, he would have made the Marquis de Sade blush. Had he been a filmmaker, he would have watched *The Human Centipede* and said "Hold my beer."

But he wasn't. He worked his magic in real life: a criminal and a sadist.

Lars, however, wasn't worried about him. The guy was going to be dead in a few moments. In fact, Lars had already set the device to subvert the man's bend, and was just waiting to have a visual before he did so.

That visual would come just as soon as the security goons managed to figure out which one of them was going to ring the doorbell. They'd been cutting straws when he left them.

Lars's mind was on something else. He was thinking of the warning they'd gotten about the assassination attempt on the Faction's leaders. Nothing had come of it. No hints, no evidence, not even a second message to say it had been called off.

And the more he considered it, the more he felt he'd been chosen for a reason. The caller could have gotten the message to anyone. They could have gone straight to the top—that much was obvious by the mere fact that they'd known his name. But they hadn't done that. They'd come to Lars.

That meant they wanted something. Something only Lars could give them.

He wondered what it was. Did they do it to set up that face-to-face meeting in the strip club, maybe get biometrics on him? Any good hacker who knew where he was could have gotten that the next time he stopped at a convenience store, just by stealing images from the security cameras.

DNA sample from a drinking glass?

Again, just follow him into a restaurant and grab the silverware when he left. No need to let him know they were even interested in him.

Lars suspected that he hadn't performed whatever task he was supposed to do. Not yet.

They'd planted a seed. Whether that task was to say something, do something, or simply answer the phone the next time they called, he didn't know. What he did know was that the Faction had wasted a ton of resources in protecting its leadership against a threat Lars didn't believe existed. Worse, the act of setting up the security might have actually called attention to some people who kept that aspect of their lives extremely well-hidden from the rest of the world. Even Lars didn't know the identity of most of the Committee.

He needed to think about this.

Finally, one of the security men marched across the road, head held high, as if he was going to show his peers that he wasn't afraid of the man who could blow his head up with a thought.

He stood before the door and pressed on the doorbell.

The mass-murderer Simon Depuis opened the door, his shock of light-brown hair instantly recognizable from the photographs.

Lars zapped him. Not at full strength—not even close to full strength—but just enough for him to crumple to the ground. Once done, Lars crossed the road, walked up the path, and stood by the door. "Thank you," he said to the security man. "That was well done."

The man saluted stiffly, and took a step back, apparently happy to let Lars take over.

Lars called into the house in Russian. No one answered, and he wondered if the animal at his feet had killed the woman he'd heard screaming earlier. If so, it made little difference to his mission, but he wished that, in all the killing he was doing, he would at least be able to save one life along the way.

He called again, waited and then sighed. "See if she's still alive," he told the man.

The guy went in. Now that the threat of a BENT who liked exploding people's heads was gone, the guy moved like a pro, smoothly clearing rooms and moving on to the next. Lars heard him head up a rickety staircase inside.

Then screams. A woman's screams.

Lars heard the stairs again, and both the screams and footsteps came closer.

The security guard was carrying a nude woman who was kicking at him and trying to beat him with her fists.

When she saw the Frenchman on the floor, a string of blood leaking from one nostril, her eyes went wide, and she went still.

The security goon kept her tight.

"Can you hear me?" Lars asked.

His voice spooked her, and she tensed. Then she looked back at the man at their feet. "Did you do this?"

"Yes. He is a menace to society."

She spat on the prone BENT. "He killed Andriy. Andriy." She kicked the man. "And then . . ." The woman sighed. "I suppose you already know what he did."

"I can imagine," Lars replied. "And I'm sorry. But I can tell you one thing. You were lucky."

She stared at him, eyes wide. "Having my husband killed and being raped by that animal is good luck?" She struggled to free her arms, and, after a nod from Lars, the security man let her go.

"Compared to what he does to most of his victims, yes. For starters, you are still alive. And young enough for that to matter. You can go on with your life."

She glared at him, then kicked the guy on the ground. He groaned.

"He's awake," the woman said, suddenly afraid again.

"He can't hurt you."

"Are you sure?"

"Yes. You see this button?" Lars showed her his phone. "It controls his bend. Right now, his power is pushing his own brain against his skull. Not hard enough to make it explode, but hard enough to cause him a hell of a lot of pain."

"And he can hear me?"

Lars shrugged. He wasn't an expert. "I suppose so."

The woman knelt beside the Frenchman and whispered something in his ear that Lars couldn't hear. Then she stood and kicked him in the nose. She kicked him again, moving from his face to his groin, where she kicked him repeatedly.

Lars exchanged a pained grimace with the security man, but said nothing. This woman hadn't deserved what happened to her, and she wasn't about to kill their man, so he let her proceed. He even lowered the pressure against the man's skull—maybe it would help him feel the woman's kicks. He was rewarded by hearing the bastard begin to whine as if in great pain. Good.

Finally, she stopped and, panting, looked up at them. "He'll never abuse a woman again," she said.

"Would you like to do the honors?" Lars asked, holding out his phone.

"What do you mean?"

"If you move this little bar over, you can increase the pressure on his head. As far as you like."

"As far? You mean . . ."

Lars nodded.

The woman grabbed the phone greedily and moved the bar slowly along its path. Blood began to pour from the Frenchman's nose. Then, from his ears. His mouth. Finally, as if afraid she'd be deprived of the main prize, she swiped the icon as far as it would go.

The Frenchman's head burst like a piece of rotten fruit.

Now, she looked down and saw that her legs were covered with gore. She seemed to remember that she was naked in front of two large men, and shrank back into herself. "I . . . can I get dressed?"

"Of course," Lars replied. "We won't annoy you anymore. You should call the police." He knew it was perfectly safe. No one would believe her about the cell phone . . . and even if they did, it wasn't a completely bad thing. Maybe it was time for the

BENT to know the fear everyone else had been living with since the 1950s.

As she closed the door, Lars thought that, perhaps, the act of getting complete revenge on the man who'd abused her might help this particular victim find closure and move on with her life.

He liked to think that he hadn't just exterminated a worthless piece of vermin, but actually done some good in the process.

He walked away. The next coordinates were fifteen miles away.

Lars didn't know how the tracking unit was locating the BENT—all he knew was that the detection apparatus was bulky and needed a team to handle it.

As long as they kept feeding him targets, he didn't really care.

Chapter 15

A week had passed since they'd returned from Siberia, and apparently, their Colombian beach retreat was still considered safe enough, because Rod hadn't relocated them.

Vernon sat on a recliner watching the turquoise sea break gently against the white sand. He'd spent most of his time right there on the chair, just sitting, staring and thinking.

His thoughts mainly concerned Maia and why she hadn't spoken to him since they returned from the mission. She seemed obsessed with Eyespy, and though she wouldn't answer any questions about the man, Vernon was convinced they'd been lovers. She hated the man with a bitterness that appeared to go beyond his criminal, sadistic, and murderous tendencies. Vernon couldn't imagine that level of venom coming from anything but a failed relationship.

Besides, he was just her type: good-looking, glib, and just about as crazy as she was.

So, it made sense that Maia was avoiding Vernon. She wouldn't want to talk about that at all.

What made less sense was that Maia appeared to be avoiding Eyespy even more assiduously. While she tolerated being in Vernon's presence, she refused to be anywhere near the other man. She would get up and leave if he entered the room, mumbling excuses that no one believed. And if Eyespy was between her and the door, Maia would simply teleport out.

Occasionally, Sarena would join Vernon, sitting the next chair over and drinking caipiroskas, a drink which she explained was exactly the same as a caipirinha, but with the cachaça replaced with vodka. Vernon tried one, and found it a little too sweet for his mood.

He didn't drink anything else, either. He knew what happened when he got drunk. He looked for solace in the arms of the nearest pretty girl. Right now, that was Sarena, and that would have been a complication, even if she had been willing. Vernon knew that two people in their shoes, broken people looking for whatever solace presented itself, could end up in bed together out of sheer boredom.

Besides, he wasn't looking for oblivion, but insight. He wanted to understand the truth about . . .

He paused to think.

. . . He didn't really know what the question was. All he knew was that he didn't have the answer, and that the sea was soothing, and that he could let his mind wander, and . . .

The princess walked slowly past. He was so zoned, he almost didn't recognize her.

Vernon jumped to his feet and ran after the tall woman. He fell into step beside her.

"Hello, princess," he said.

She turned her head and peered at him. "Hello, Vernon," she said dully.

"I haven't seen you in days."

"I've been in my cabin." She shook her head. "I had water in there. But now I'm hungry. I came out to get food. No use in dying of starvation and leaving my people without any leader at all, is there?"

"Do you mind if I join you?" Vernon said.

"I was planning on just asking for a sandwich at the bar and eating it in my room. I'm not sure I'm ready for people just yet."

With most women, Vernon would have insisted. He would have been convinced that they were just trying to call attention to themselves. But not with the princess; her quiet dignity made such thoughts impossible. "I'll walk you there, then."

She shook her head slightly, about to refuse, but then paused. "I suppose that's for the best. I . . . I'm quite weak."

Resisting the urge to take her by the shoulder—he suspected she wouldn't want that, wouldn't feel comfortable being treated like an invalid—Vernon walked by her side, ready to jump into action if she faltered.

They made it to the bar without incident, and the princess asked for a toasted ham and cheese sandwich, which came in little triangles with mayonnaise in them. Then they turned back toward her little hut.

Vernon stopped at the door. The curtains were drawn, but the glow of the sun hitting the windows seeped through them, suffusing the room in soft orange tones. "Please let me know if you need anything," he said.

The princess took a step into the room, then stopped.

"You know what? I don't think I want to go back in there. Why don't you get yourself something, and we can sit at that table?"

Vernon nodded, walked back to the bar, and bought a bag of chipá bread and a coke. Not knowing what the princess preferred to drink, he brought her bottled water.

He tried to make it look like he wasn't hurrying, but the anxiety that she might change her mind was hard to resist.

"That was very thoughtful of you," the princess said when Vernon awkwardly handed her the bottle of water. "Thank you."

"You're welcome."

Each cabin had a little table with two chairs of the typical outdoors type in which plastic strips made up the sitting surface and the seatback, and everything was held up by a chromed metal frame. The table was round with a glass top.

"I'm sorry about what happened," Vernon said after they'd both taken a bite of their food. "He seemed like an admirable man."

"He was," she replied. "A great man in an unfair situation. He should have been leading people to better themselves, organizing great deeds in the name of our tribe." Then she shrugged. "But he always did what he could to help people."

"If we manage to stop the Faction, he might have made a difference in more people's lives than almost anyone else. You, too."

"But now, I'm out of the game."

Vernon looked down at his feet. "Yeah. I know. I can't imagine what it must be like, losing the person closest to you and also losing your bend. I admire that you simply stayed inside and gave yourself time to grieve. I wouldn't have been so measured. Hell, I wasn't so measured. When I lost my wife . . ."

The princess nodded. "We all know. Rod briefed us. And he also told us we could trust you with our lives. I saw what you did when my brother died. No warrior of our people would have avenged him as quickly and thoroughly as you did. You did him honor."

"The honor is mine. I'm not worthy to avenge a prince," Vernon replied.

"A prince on paper only."

"I saw how he acted. I'll always remember him as a prince."

"You're very sweet to say that. And now, I'm a princess without a power. All I can do is help finance things . . . but Rod doesn't seem to need any money. We tried to wire him some, but he refused. Wouldn't even give us a crypto address."

"He probably thinks someone can track him through that," Vernon said.

"If Rod thinks that, it's probably because he's already done it to someone."

"Yeah," Vernon said.

They ate in silence for a few minutes before Vernon, unable to cope with the quiet, asked. "Do you think you'll be all right?"

"No. I think I'm going to be hurting for a long time," the princess replied. "A long time."

"Yeah, I know. It's been four years for me, and I still want to kill people and break things." He looked at her, the calm demeanor, the serene look. "You have no idea how much I admire you."

The princess chuckled. "It's all training, you know."

"What?"

"Training. I was brought up to act like a royal by parents who were subjects—important subjects—of the British crown. My religion, apart from the worship of an ancestor god called Bomazi, is that of stiff-upper-lip. But it's all a façade. When my brother fell, they tore something out of me. Everything that made me human was gone in an instant. I could have howled at the moon, I could have let myself die. If I'd had the strength to do it, I would have killed everyone in that prison: the guards, the inmates, our strike force . . . and me. It would have felt right, and it would have been precisely what I wanted." She shook her head. "But my physical strength died with James."

Vernon was so shocked that he blurted his response before thinking. "His name was James?"

She contemplated him for a moment, then chuckled ruefully. "You aren't the right person to confide deep thoughts to, are you?"

"I'm sorry," he said. "I don't know what I was thinking. You must think I'm a complete jackass." He stood to leave.

Her hand on his arm, the lightest of light touches, stopped him. "No." She grinned, the first real expression of anything but quiet sorrow she'd seen from her. "I mean, you are a bit of a jackass, but your heart is in the right place, and I appreciate you taking this time with me. It means a lot. Please sit."

"Thank you," he said, not meeting her eyes.

"Yes, his name was James. My parents thought the British were the greatest people ever to grace the planet. Perhaps, in my parents' time, that was true."

"Colonialists."

"True. And men who believed that might was right. But also men who brought with them enlightenment that displaced superstition and laws that replaced barbarism with enlightenment. If you took them as a concept and not as fallible individuals, you could understand my parents' outlook. Also, both my father and my brother went to Eton. My father went there when it was the place where all the future leaders of the Empire were educated. And both my brother and I went to Oxford—he read political science, and I read computer science. In fact, I went all the way through the doctoral program. That's where the leaders of today are formed, and don't let anyone tell you differently."

"Wow. Don't go anywhere near a university today. The students will stone you for saying that. Elitist imperialist capitalism. Or something like that."

"I'm a philanthropic black woman from Africa," she said with a mischievous grin. "I could tell them that the sky is orange and that there's a conspiracy of mutant toads trying to take over the world, and none of them would dare speak out against me."

"Wow," Vernon said. "You're a cynic."

She pulled herself straight, composed her features, and gave him a stern look. "Please remember your place, young man."

It was like a bucket of ice water thrown over his head. He leaned back in his chair, studying the princess. She held his gaze impassively. "You're shitting me, aren't you?" he asked hesitantly, after a long moment.

The princess sighed. "That's a relief," she said. "For a moment, I wasn't sure you'd catch on. You'd be surprised at how many don't."

"You mean all your aloofness, the royal untouchability . . ."

"It's pretty much an act. Yes. I think James mainly did it to impress the girls. And I did it because if I didn't, I would have looked like the rebellious younger princess nobody can control. That is like the oldest cliché in the book. So, I played along. It allowed me to only let the people I chose get close to me, which was an advantage at times."

Vernon shook his head. "You certainly had me fooled."

"That's the whole point. Anyway, I see you're too much of a gentleman to ask, so I'll tell you. My name is Elizabeth."

"James and Elizabeth."

"Yes. My father admired the British, but he wasn't very well-versed on their religious history, which makes me wonder what exactly they were teaching him at Eton."

Vernon chuckled. "And I thought you were an ice princess."

"Not with people I like."

The food was long since consumed, and Elizabeth stood. "I think I'll volunteer to help Rod's programmers talk to that Brain you stole. It might make me feel a little less useless. Of course, I probably know more about the way computers work than any of those hacks." She sighed. "But first, I want to go to bed for a little bit. I'm still not recovered, and I suspect I won't be all right for a longish time. But I feel better than I did, and I have you to thank for that."

Looking into her beautiful brown eyes, Vernon almost begged to be invited inside.

Almost.

"Get some rest," he said, standing up and nodding to her. "Just be sure to let me know if you need anything."

"Thank you," Elizabeth replied. Then she disappeared into the room.

Chapter 16

The space, a tiny prefab unit abandoned by an Argentine Antarctic expedition a decade earlier, was jammed full of people.

"Norway and now Antarctica," Vernon said, rubbing his hands together. "Don't these people know there are warm places in the world?"

Eyespy grunted. "You should try living in a prison in Siberia before you complain. Those guys didn't even know the meaning of turning on the heat."

"People," Winnie-the-Pooh, this time mounted on a large flatscreen TV, said. "This is unproductive."

"I agree," Vernon said. "It feels like we've been sitting in staging areas waiting to attack hidden facilities ever since you came back into our lives. It's starting to get repetitive."

"It's all been building up to this," Rod replied. "Today, we'll be making the world safe again, and taking this murderous tech away from people who shouldn't have it. Once we knock over this facility, it will just be a question of killing the men with the portable devices, but the Norwegian Faction will no longer have a chance to kill the BENT on a massive scale."

No one argued with him this time. Every internet site, every social stream, every television news channel was covered in information about the wholesale murder of BENT using their own bend against them. Hundreds, perhaps thousands had been murdered already, and the rate was increasing daily.

Rod looked around the room, including the hacker team—and Elizabeth—around a cluster of monitors. "Are you ready for what you have to do?"

Everyone nodded.

"Maia?" Rod asked.

"Let's get this over with," she replied.

"Do you have the Brain?" Rod asked.

Vernon opened a pocket on his utility belt to reveal the cylinder. The mass of cables had been replaced. Now it only sported an antenna—which allowed the programmers to give it instructions— a portable battery, and a USB cable that would allow it to be plugged into any computer they were likely to encounter.

"Excellent. Good luck."

They clasped hands with Maia, and they blinked into an enemy installation.

Again.

The room they appeared in was just that: a room, and Vernon let out a sigh of relief. He'd half-expected Eyespy's reconnaissance to be as cursory and half-assed as everything else he did, which made Vernon expect to appear in the middle of a block of ice or ancient submerged granite formation. The fact that there was a room here at all was cause for major celebration.

Even better was that the room was precisely what you'd expect from a recently-constructed secret facility: polished concrete floors, walls, and ceilings gleaming in fluorescent light.

"Ah," Maia said. "An empty room. Such a threat."

Eyespy glared at her, but he seemed to feel the scorn. Vernon could tell that whatever history existed between these two, it was more complicated than Maia had let on, and even more than Vernon had sniffed out. They were tangled worse than a Shakespeare comedy of mistaken identities . . . and made about as much sense. "Next time, I'll be sure to have you drop us in a spot full of surveillance electronics and people. Would that make you happy?"

"Ecstatic," Maia replied. "Now, I suppose I'll have to walk this whole huge tunnel with you to make sure I'm on hand when everything goes tits-up and you have to run away in a hurry. I had enough of that back in Siberia."

"This isn't getting us anywhere," the princess said. She'd come along for the ride because she insisted that if they needed to plug the Brain into anything, and it wasn't cooperating, they would need her to intervene.

Vernon suspected she was secretly looking to get herself killed and avoid all that messy healing in her future. And he was grimly determined to prevent it.

"Where do we go now?" the princess asked.

Eyespy glanced at a wall. "There's a hallway just outside this door. The first two rooms opening on both sides of it are empty. Then there's a storeroom full of bags of concrete and things like that. A couple of offices. Following that, the complex bends in a L-shape." He turned his head so his magic eyes could follow the path and continued speaking. "The hallway goes on for a bit, and that's when we come to the first of the containment doors. We'll need to jump past that one. There's no one in the segment behind it. After that, there's another length of hall and another containment door before we find any people. I see fourteen guys working on the equipment in the big room. Also, my sight is getting fuzzy there, which means the place is full of really crappy radiation." He cocked his head and squinted. "Oh, those imbeciles. All of them are dotted with little cancer nodules. I wonder if they knew it was a suicide mission when they started."

"Fourteen," Vernon said. "Good. "How many have guns?"

"Two guards in the room. Another six at the exit—two on duty, two resting—which is all the way on the other side of the complex," Eyespy replied. "Piece of cake."

"So, we just jump into the machine room, take out the guards, and force the scientists to show us what's important?" Vernon asked.

Eyespy shrugged. "Actually, Vern, with a cakewalk like this one, I'm not really concerned about how we do it, as long as I get to walk when it's done." He grinned at Maia. "Want to come with? I promise you wild times and a lot of revenge. I'm going to make life hell for the guys who tossed me in The Hole, but if you like, we can fry the fuckers who cut your little sister to pieces on the way. Make it your fee for moving me around."

"Does everyone have a weapon?" the princess asked.

Vernon, Maia, and Sarena held up the compact machine pistols they'd been assigned. Eyespy shrugged. "I left mine in the cabin," he said. "But I don't really need one."

"All right. Then give Maia the coordinates to the room."

"Coordinates? I can't do that without the GPS stuff we used to pinpoint this room. We'll need to jump through."

"Very well," Elizabeth replied. "Lead the way."

The door opened without complaint, leading to a hallway that was just as described. They walked down the corridor, turned right, and found the curtain.

"Just jump through this one," Eyespy indicated. "The hall continues on the other side."

Maia took them across. Then she held up a hand. "Wait," she said. "That blast door, how thick is it?"

Eyespy shrugged and looked at the offending partition for a moment. "About four feet," he replied.

"Damn. What are they trying to contain?"

"Radiation for sure. We'll find out what else when we get there, won't we?" Eyespy replied. They walked again, and when they reached another blast door apparently identical to the first, he studied the room beyond. "All right. They've moved around a bit. The scientists are all on the left side of the room where there appears to be a bank of equipment. They're not armed. One of the guards is all the way to the far end, while another is off on the right. There also appears to be a guy in the bathroom, but he doesn't have any weapons with him."

Sarena's clothes dropped to the ground, and she disappeared from view. Only a black weapon floating in the air gave her presence away.

"Your pistol is showing," Eyespy said. But his eyes were twitching, as if searching for any sign of the missing woman. Vernon smiled. All Sarena had to do was drop the gun, and Eyespy wouldn't see her. He enjoyed seeing Eyespy thwarted.

"I'll take the guard to the right," Sarena said.

"And I'll do the one at the back. I can kill him without shooting, and before he even knows he's under attack, which will minimize the damage to the equipment," Eyespy said.

"Look at you being all socially responsible," Maia said.

"I don't care about the damage, Maia," Eyespy replied. "I just want to turn everything over to Rod in one piece so I don't owe that fucker anything." He turned to the group. "There's an open space with no people or equipment about three meters from where we're standing. I'll give you a mark for the next jump." As the team put their hands together, Eyespy watched intently. "Three, two, one . . . Now!"

They appeared in the room.

A second later, an alarm began to wail.

A moment after that, the guard in the back of the room screamed and fell to the floor.

The second guard managed to get off a single shot before a burst from Sarena's machine gun cut him in half.

The scientists looked up from their consoles without much alarm. Roughly half of them were men, the other half women—and all of them were equally pale and stooped.

"Don't move," Vernon said, brandishing a machine gun.

"Why would we move?" a woman asked. "Why would we defend this place?" She might have been attractive once, and her bearing denoted that she must have had authority; she had tried to pull herself up to her full height when she spoke to them. Ultimately, however, the pain in her body won, and she stooped once more. "We don't want to be here. We just want to go. Those men you killed forced us to work. We're not stupid. We know what the radiation is doing to us."

Another man stepped forward. "Here, we'll show you what we've been doing. We'll tell you how it all works. It will be such a relief to know that our toil won't be used for evil by those—"

A sudden scream filled the room, and another scientist staggered out from behind a bank of computers. He caromed off a computer and tried to grab a steel rack but was unable to grip it with nerveless fingers, and then fell to the floor. A metal rod of some sort protruded from his back, and a crimson blossom was spreading over his white smock.

"He was trying to break something. With this." A fire axe floated into the air and then was carelessly tossed onto the dead man's back.

"So . . . trying to distract us while your companion destroyed what we came here for?" Maia asked.

"Now!" the woman scientist shouted.

The scientists broke into two groups. Half of them charged at the BENT, while the other half attacked the equipment.

The only one who didn't move was the woman who'd given the command. She stood there, mouth still open after shouting the order. A moment later, steam emerged from her nostrils, and then she toppled to one side.

"Bitch," Eyespy said as he turned his deadly eyes to the next target.

Vernon shook himself out of his shock and lunged for the computers. Two men attempted to stop him, but he ignored them except to press his hand to their faces. They reeled away, screaming.

A woman was attempting to do something complicated on a menu screen, desperately typing commands to erase the evidence of creating weapons with the capacity to commit genocide against a full 15 percent of the world's population.

Vernon put his hands around her neck and heard the sizzle as her skin came into contact with his. Then he simply brought his hands together, not squeezing, but allowing the chemical factory in his epidermis to cut through skin, muscle, bone.

When he pulled his hands away, the woman's head fell to the floor.

Gunfire erupted behind him, and Vernon turned to see two men fall to Elizabeth's weapon. Ricochets echoed through the room, bullets pinging against the concrete and the metal of the accoutrements until the sound died down.

All of the scientists had been killed.

"What do we do now?" Maia said.

"There's still the guy in the bathroom," Eyespy reminded them. "He's trying to be very, very quiet. Hasn't even got his pants up." He looked over at Vernon and gave him a nasty grin. "Want to walk in there and invite him to join us?"

"That won't be necessary," Elizabeth replied. "Just give me the Brain and keep an eye on the guy in the loo."

Vernon pulled it off his belt and handed it to her. Elizabeth carried it to the nearest computer, plugged in the USB, and moved a mouse to wake up the computer. A password prompt appeared, and the princess waited.

Within moments, the prompt disappeared again, and a screen came on.

"Ready," a voice came over the speaker.

"Good work," Elizabeth said. "Do you have control?"

"Oh, yes. The security here was laughable. How they haven't been hacked is a mystery."

"I think it's because they've never turned on the antenna, which means they're physically separate from every network on the planet . . . and I doubt a lot of hackers are going to come all this way to find out what's on the drive. Not with armed guards on the premises." Elizabeth turned back to the rest of the group. "We've got control of every computer in this complex. We're opening the antennas to transmission to let Rod into . . ."

Every screen in the room went on, and Winnie-the-Pooh looked down at them. "Hello, everyone," Rod said. "Color me impressed. You left ten minutes ago."

"We're good at what we do," Maia replied. "Can we go now?"

"By all means," the bears said, speaking in unison from a dozen places. "Go."

Maia winked out of existence.

"Where did she go?" Vernon asked. "We need her to get us out of here!"

The image of the Pooh Bear shrugged a hundred times like something in a funhouse mirror. "How should I know? Probably into the middle of the sun, or out in space somewhere. The device doesn't allow for really fine control. It just lets you send her waaay out somewhere."

"Wait . . . you . . .?"

"Yep."

Beside Vernon, Eyespy collapsed, nauseous vapor spewing from every orifice in his head.

"And I can also turn it inward," the bear said, then shrugged again. "Although Eyespy probably wasn't a good dude, so no one will be too shocked at his death. Which leaves me with you, Vernon. Feeling all tingly? That's your skin eating away at the flesh beneath it. I guess it's poetic justice, in a way . . . you're feeling what so many of your victims did."

The burning intensified. The Pooh Bear looked down on him, expressionless as only a cartoon can be.

Vernon clenched his teeth. It *burned.*

Then he screamed through clenched teeth.

His entire body was fire. He could tell with pinpoint accuracy where his most sensitive regions—the ones with the most nerve endings—were located, because those were the regions that hurt most.

He screamed again. Somehow, he'd fallen to the floor. He didn't even notice it. Movement flickered in the room. He didn't care. He just screamed.

Vernon knew he was already dead, knew his skin must already be burned to a crisp. He just wanted the pain to stop.

Then the lights went out, and he screamed into the darkness.

Chapter 17

Vernon supposed his skin had burned through his eyelids and into his eyeballs. Blindness might actually be a boon, since he wouldn't be able to see the wreck of his body.

Except . . . he lay there trying to figure out what might debunk that conclusion.

Finally, he realized that the pain had actually disappeared.

Which probably just meant that his skin had finished chewing through his nerves, and that he would be dying soon.

It was quite pleasant. It was warm, it was dark. No need to worry.

A hand shook his shoulder. A light made him blink.

"Wha . . ." he said.

"Oh, thank God. You're all right." Even in the dark, he recognized Elizabeth's husky tones.

"I don't think I'm going anywhere," he replied. He moved his hand to show her the damage. The cellphone light showed pink, new skin. "What?"

"Looks like your skin has been working to replace your . . . other skin, I guess." She pulled him to his feet. "We need to get out of here. I hope you can walk, because carrying you out isn't as easy for me as it was before my brother died."

To Vernon's surprise, he found that he could walk without pain. "Wow," he said. "Why did he stop?"

For the nonce, he set aside the much more important question of why the hell Rod had betrayed them. They'd done everything he asked. They'd been a brilliant team.

"The Brain disconnected the power. That turned off the device."

It took Vernon a moment to grasp what she was referring to. Then he remembered the hard drive in the cylinder.

"Why would a computer do that?" he asked.

"Because it's not a computer. It's an extremely sophisticated AI. It's actually conscious, most likely a dozen times more self-aware than Turing-level. And it likes me."

"What?"

"The assholes"—in her cultured tones, the word somehow sounded like the worst insult possible—"that Rod had studying it were too dumb to realize what they were dealing with and too coarse to avoid poking at it and trying to tear it down. The first thing I did when I joined the team was to install buffers against their prodding. The hackers were too stupid to recognize them, but Juin knew exactly what I did. So now, it looked out for me."

"You gave it a name?"

"No. I just asked it what its name was," Elizabeth said. She hoisted the cylinder. "I told you. It's alive and aware."

They'd reached the far wall, when Vernon remembered something. "There's a dude in the bathroom."

"Just leave him there," she replied. "We really need to get out of here."

It wasn't a fast process. Lit only by the cellphone flashlight, the dark corridors took on a more menacing aspect. Worse still, they had to melt through two blast doors that mirrored the ones they'd used to enter.

At the first, Vernon hesitated, wondering if his skin, so recently burned and regenerated, would be up to the task. Indeed, he wondered if it would ever work again.

"Well?" the princess asked.

He swallowed and laid his hand on the cold metal. Only when it began to dissolve did he breathe again.

After the second door, Vernon made to advance up the hall, but the princess put a hand on his shoulder. "Didn't Eyespy say something about guards?"

"Yeah," Vernon responded grimly. "There's supposed to be four more of them. Maybe six—I wasn't paying that much attention—between us and the exit door. And they're probably wondering why the lights suddenly went out. And also why the emergency lights didn't kick in afterward."

A harsh voice shouted from the back end of the hall in a language Vernon couldn't identify.

"And there they are. Try to stay behind me if you can," he told the princess.

"Don't be ridiculous," she whispered back. Out loud, she shouted something in what sounded like the same language. The terror she put into her voice made Vernon think she must have taken acting classes. You could almost feel it in your bones.

The man shouted back.

She answered, and ended with a scream.

Vernon heard the sound of footsteps moving quickly in the opposite direction.

"What did you tell them?" Vernon said.

"That we had a containment leak, and that it had broken through the blast doors. I also told them to run as far from this facility as they could get."

"I hope they believed you."

"From what I saw in there, it would be a good idea for them to do so. Did you see the warning labels on some of those canisters?" she asked. "It's a good thing we didn't hit most of them when we were shooting at guards."

"I seem to recall it was you doing most of the shooting," he pointed out.

"Which was lucky, seeing what the rest of you would likely have done."

They reached a suite of rooms that showed signs of having been hastily abandoned, then arrived at a stairway leading up.

Vernon looked at it skeptically. "That is a beautiful place to set up an ambush," he said.

"Then you go first. You're the indestructible one."

"Grenades are bad for my ears. And that's how I'd attack us. Grenades."

"Look. It's not like we have any choice. Maia isn't here . . ." Her voice trailed off.

Vernon put a foot on the first step. "Yeah. I know. Come on."

He trudged listlessly in the direction of the frozen wastes above them, while Elizabeth followed in silence. There was no real reason to hurry. There was no one coming to get them, and it was going to be a long walk across some really icy terrain.

He wondered how he was going to get his skin to create nutrients and shelter for Elizabeth, but he supposed all he had to do was to think about it, and his skin would do it.

Ten floors up, and still, the stairs—a concrete snail through the frozen rock—rose. Vernon felt relief to note that he felt perfectly energized, and that extra oxygen reached his blood via his skin. Despite the evidence at the doors, he'd been worried that the attack by Rod would have damaged something irrevocably.

Finally, up above them, a rectangle of color could be seen. A light gray that teased the presence of the sun.

Five minutes later, they emerged into a wan light. No more than an hour had passed since they left the hut. Unfortunately, that hut, though also in Antarctica, was on the Peninsula, seven hundred miles away. It was still about four in the morning—but in the Antarctic summer, that meant that the pale light of day was already present.

He poked his head out the entrance, gave a cursory glance, then returned. There was no sign of the guards.

"Which way?" he asked, huddled in the exit door, which he saw had been concealed by a hinged plastic cover in the shape of an iceberg. It wouldn't have fooled anyone inspecting it closely, but that wasn't its purpose; it would have been invisible from the air.

"North," Elizabeth replied.

"And which way is that?"

"I assume pretty much every direction is north from here," she replied.

Vernon thought about it for a second before groaning. "Are you actually making bad jokes at a time like this?"

"Would you prefer for me to moan that I'm going to die in a few hours?" Her face turned serious. "Let's face it. I'm not remotely dressed for a jaunt across Antarctica. And even if I was, so were Scott and his men. I'm as good as dead, and my only option—also a very bad one—is to wait here for the Faction to return."

"What about Rod?"

"He has what he wants. The Brain managed to beam everything up to him before we realized he was part of the problem and not the solution. On the other hand . . . the Faction won't be an issue. The Brain sent every single document in the facility to Interpol, the CIA, the FBI, the FSB, the Guóānbù, and every other security service on the planet. That's a wealth of files, histories, articles, and research logs, enough to put every member of that organization behind bars."

"Did Rod order that?"

"No. I did."

"How?" Vernon asked.

Elizabeth looked away from him and pointed to her ear, which sported a tiny earbud which he hadn't noticed. "I can talk to the Brain through this jack. Unfortunately, it isn't much help with the limited range on its antenna . . . and especially not with the nearest wi-fi network five hundred miles away. It can't do much in the physical universe."

"Too bad. And if we go back inside? Can we call for help?"

"Maybe. Depends on whether they have the fuses and wiring we'll need to replace the stuff the Brain burned out."

"In any case," a new voice said, "it's a moot point, because you're coming with us."

Two men had stepped into view. The one who spoke was a tall, slightly rotund man with a black fur-lined jacket whose hood covered his face. The one who hadn't spoken was a soldier in a full winter camouflage, complete with rifle and whitecoat. The rifle was pointed straight at Elizabeth, painting her forehead with a red laser dot.

"Mr. Pandor," the man went on. "Please don't try to be a hero. My companion has orders to shoot Her Royal Highness if you move. Besides, I can kill you as well. I have a device that can turn your skin into an acid bath. I implore you not to force me to use it."

Vernon shuddered, remembering what Rod had done to him. He raised his hands slowly, and Elizabeth did the same.

"Good start. Now, I'd like you to step out of the stairwell. Again, let's take this slowly. The princess first, if you don't mind."

Vernon followed Elizabeth from out of the hole. Moments later, he stood on the windswept Antarctic plain, wondering how the hell he'd missed the platoon of soldiers that appeared to surround them.

A moment later, he had his answer. The stairs were set into an incline, a soft hill that rose gently for a hundred meters, then fell away in a cliff. White against white made it impossible to see that there was an enormous shelf where a large ski-plane had landed.

He only saw it when they were marched into the plain.

The bodies of several men lay there, bodies stitched with bullet holes.

"The guards?"

The talkative member of the team that had captured them nodded. "They knew much too much," he said from within his hood.

"So do we," Elizabeth pointed out.

"Then we'll need to give each other mutual guarantees of some sort. You see, I need your help in the most desperate way, and I need you to trust me, because I really, really don't have the time to find more people with the information I need if you two happen to die on me during torture. So, how can I make you believe I won't kill you, so that you will cooperate?"

"Not an easy task," Elizabeth said.

"How about you give me the device that can kill me?" Vernon asked.

"You know I can't do that," the man replied.

"All right. I'll start smaller. How about you tell us who the fuck you are?"

The man pulled back his hood to reveal a completely bald, pale head. Vernon recognized him as the guy from the video who'd murdered Rod's ghost. "You can call me Lars."

Chapter 18

The airplane was divided into two compartments. The rear—through which they entered—had two canvas benches on either side, on which the soldiers sat. Crates lashed down with belts occupied the center aisle. The front, just aft of the flight deck, held a lounge-like space, complete with leather couches and a drinks cabinet.

The lounge had its own stewardess.

"Hell," Vernon said, looking around. "This almost makes me want to join the Faction. As an officer, of course."

Lars smiled thinly. "I don't think you'd be welcome." He looked around. "But if it makes you feel any better, this plane doesn't belong to the Faction at all. It belongs to the Heller Group, which is a mercenary organization only loosely connected to us. And the Faction didn't even rent it. I did, from my own funds . . . which, I admit, came mostly from the Faction. But they're unlikely to miss them."

"Why?" Elizabeth asked.

"Before I answer that, can I ask you to give me your promise not to try to attack me?" Lars said.

"I don't have much choice. I've seen—and felt—what that thing can do," Vernon replied.

"I propose to put the control in my pocket. But only if you promise me not to attack as soon as my back is turned."

"You'd trust us?" Vernon asked.

"Yes. My problem with you isn't that I find you untrustworthy," Lars replied.

"It's with our very existence," Vernon spat back. Then he sighed. "Whatever. I promise I won't kill you. Or even try to hurt you, unless you start it."

"That's good enough for me." Lars put his phone in his pocket.

Vernon shook his head in disbelief. "How are you even still alive?" he asked.

"Why? Are you going to break your word?" Lars responded.

"No . . . but almost anyone else would have. In a second. In less than a second. Hell, most of the BENTs I know would have murdered you on general principles the second you put away the phone."

"And yet you didn't. Why?"

"Because I'm stupid that way," Vernon said. "I've got a lot of blood on my hands, but most of it was taken in the heat of the moment. I've killed and ruined dozens of people—and I'll admit that most of them deserved it less than you do—but I did it either in self-defense or to avenge what happened to my wife. I know I *should* kill you. But I won't."

"That's comforting," Lars replied. "And, to give the devil his due, it's also quite honorable of you. It's one of those things that makes what I do so difficult."

"It doesn't seem you're having much difficulty. I got to watch you kill a man firsthand. You enjoyed it," Elizabeth said. "And you would have enjoyed doing it to me, too. And to him."

Lars shrugged. "I never said I was perfect. I've sold my soul to a cause. I believe in that cause fervently. Passionately. I know deep within my soul that the only solution for the problem of BENT is to kill you all. It's the only way people like me, normal people, can ever survive. I know, sometimes, the people I kill are good people who don't deserve it. I'm not stupid. There's honor in enemies, just as in friends. But that's not something you can stop to think about in the middle of a war."

"Not everyone is at war," Elizabeth said.

"Yes," Lars replied. "They are. On one side, we have the BENT, who, whether they want it or not, are making baseline humans obsolete. Look at Quake, or any of the heroes. And yes, the villains, too. Their confrontations take place one level above what regular people can aspire to. We're already on our way to irrelevance. Soon, there will be nothing but BENTs."

"That won't happen. Eighty-five percent of humanity is still born without a bend. Even to BENT-BENT couples. Do you think they'll let their kids die off?"

"Not die off. They'll probably kill them. Like in Sparta, leaving them to die of exposure somehow. Or worse."

"Worse?"

"My nightmare scenario isn't that the BENT kill all the baseline people. It's that they keep them alive to breed them and select that 15 percent of the offspring worthy to be nurtured. But I don't think that will happen. I think evolution will take its course, and eventually, the BENT mutation, whatever it is, will become dominant and survive, while normality will end."

"You don't have children, do you?" Elizabeth asked.

"No, but I don't see what difference it makes."

"If you had a child and knew there was a 15 percent chance of it being BENT, you wouldn't be discussing the possibility of killing us all. And you'd know that a BENT mother would never allow her normal child to be killed for not being BENT."

Lars gave her a hard look. "People are a product of the society they live in. Mothers no less than anyone else. Do you think there were no mothers in Sparta?" His pale features had grown flushed, and perspiration ran down his forehead.

"All right. We're not going to agree on this one," Vernon said. "What are we doing here?"

"As I said on the ice, we have a common enemy."

Vernon and Elizabeth exchanged looks. Finally, Elizabeth spoke. "Except you haven't told us who it is."

"It's the man who attacked you in the complex. My men found a dead BENT there. Quite a famous one, in fact: Eyespy. He hadn't been killed by the guards. And he hadn't been melted by you," he nodded toward Vernon. "Which would indicate he'd been attacked by the device being developed in the lab."

"Which says nothing."

"In fact, it says quite a bit, to me, at least. I believe the person we're looking for is a functionary of the Norwegian Faction," Lars said.

"Bullshit," Vernon said. "You're fishing."

"I'm not. I have other evidence."

"Listen," Vernon said. "I know what you're thinking. You're thinking we'll be so happy that you pulled our asses out of the freezer back there that we'll tell you everything about the operation. Well, you're out of luck. Just drop us at the first place with an airport, and we'll call it even."

"It doesn't sound even to me. I saved you from a long, cold"—he glanced at Elizabeth—"and eventually lonely walk. But what have you done for me?"

"We've listened to your rants," Vernon replied.

Elizabeth held up a hand. "Vernon, why are you protecting him?" she asked.

Vernon knew who she was referring to. Rod. "Because I want to strangle him with my own two hands. Besides, he's one of ours."

"Are you sure?" Elizabeth asked.

"Of course I'm sure. He's been with us since the beginning. On and off, but Maia and I know him well."

"Do you, really? So, can you tell me what he looks like? What his bend is?" Elizabeth spoke gently, almost apologetically.

"It's obviously some king of computer power," Vernon replied. "Superspeed processing or something."

"Or something?"

"Dammit. What are you saying? That the man who's been trying to stop the Faction all his life is just a baseline human? Well, even if he is, he's one of the good guys." Vernon glared at her. "And as such, I reserve the right to kill him myself without interference."

"I postulate that he isn't BENT," Lars said. "And I suspect he isn't against the Faction. He's part of a political division within the group."

"And you? Which side are you on?" Vernon asked.

"I . . . I guess you'd call me the Minister of War. That's not my official title, you understand, it's just the way I think of myself. I am the highest-ranking member of the Norwegian Faction's Committee whose role is purely in the field. As such, my job is to execute the will of the more sedentary elements of our leadership." His gaze hardened. "But since they appear to be at war with one another, I have decided to impose my own will."

"That's insane," Vernon said. "But then again, so is everything else about you guys, so it's not exactly a surprise."

Lars sighed. "I suppose I'd see it the same way in your position."

The stewardess whispered in Lars's ear. He stood and said, "Excuse me. I have a message. I will leave the device here. Please don't try to disable it . . . you might set it off, and I don't think you want that."

He disappeared into the cabin.

Five minutes later, he returned, face even more pale than his original past color. "I'm afraid I just received some distressing news, which I assume you already know about. It appears someone has leaked everything about the Faction to certain authorities, including names and places. While I am not on that particular list, it will change the power dynamic considerably."

"Oopsies," Elizabeth said with a shrug.

Lars glared at her, then laughed. "Look. I want to make something clear. I find the BENT personally disgusting, and more than that, I find you threatening and disturbing. But I understand how, from your point of view, I'm the bad guy, and why you might find this funny. I get it." His gaze went from one to the other. "Now, look at it from my point of view. I live in a world where no amount of effort, no amount of work, no amount of money, even, can make up for the fact that there are people out there who can lift buildings with one hand, or create earthquakes on command, or just walk into any vault on the planet and take whatever wealth doesn't belong to them. We needed an equalizer, something to keep the balance, to bring the other side to the negotiating table."

"That isn't what you planned to use it for," Vernon pointed out.

"No. It wasn't. I explained my reasons. You can think of me as a monster if you like, but I feel I'm still correct. I still wish we'd succeeded. But at least I know this will bring about a better balance. Now, the BENT will need us. If your enemy is in possession of one of these devices, then no one but a regular human without a bend will serve to fight that enemy."

"Do you think the government agencies who know about this will allow the tech to get widely used? Every government has their BENT special forces, and no one wants to give terrorists an edge," Vernon said. "It will get locked up with the nukes and the chemical weapons and the other WMDs."

"It doesn't matter what they want," Lars replied. He gave them a sad smile. "The genie is out of the bottle. Too many people know, thanks to you."

"So, where are you taking us?" Vernon asked.

To his surprise, it was Elizabeth who answered. "Mexico City," she replied.

Lars raised an eyebrow. "That is a strange guess," he said. "As strange as it is inaccurate. This plane will refuel in the Azores and land in a city in Norway called Hammerfest. We'll be meeting with some people there, and deciding what to do next."

"Actually, no," Elizabeth said. "We're going to Mexico City. We've got just enough fuel to make it, and—"

This time, the person who interrupted the conversation wasn't the stewardess, but a man in a pilot's uniform.

"Excuse me, sir," the man said, addressing Lars, "I have some disturbing news."

Then he leaned over and whispered something into Lars's ear.

Chapter 19

"You?" Lars's eyes went wide, and he turned back to the BENT. "You hijacked my plane? How?"

Vernon stared back, trying to keep a poker face when, in fact, he was just as surprised as Lars was.

"With a little help from a cybernetic friend," Elizabeth replied. "And hijack is a little too strong a word," Elizabeth said. "We're taking you where you need to be. You want to catch the man who destroyed your organization, right?"

"Of course. But we'll need weeks of preparation, online searches for his footprints. Surveillance. I imagine this isn't someone who will just walk up and down the street proclaiming that he was the man who brought down the Norwegian Faction."

"I already know who he is. And I know where he will be. So, if you want to catch him, you'd best listen to me."

"Do I have a choice?" Lars asked. "The pilot says not one electronic system is responding to his attempts to control the plane. He says these modern planes don't have a full manual mode, only computer-assist that can't be turned off. He's tried cutting everything off, but apparently, the manufacturers consider the electronics a safety feature. So, I can either accept we're going to Mexico City, or I can kill you. I really don't want to kill you, so I'll listen."

"You wouldn't kill us just to do what you wanted? What happened to 'Every BENT must die'?" Elizabeth asked.

Lars sighed. "I don't like killing people I know, especially when there's little to be gained. I'm a practical man. I've accepted that what the Faction was trying to do is no longer viable. The things that have been revealed are going to cause an international uproar, and there's no way we can do what we'd originally planned. People will lynch anyone using one of our devices. So . . . I'll have to be satisfied with the knowledge that at least now the method to control the BENT exists. Who knows? It might be better this way. Here, take the device if you want. I won't use it." Lars kicked the briefcase in their direction.

"Good," Elizabeth said. She smiled. "Because you couldn't have used it anyway. The first thing the Brain did after hacking the airplane's network was to turn off your device."

"You mean I could have melted him into a pool of goo?" Vernon asked. "Dammit."

Elizabeth grinned. "You don't want to kill him."

"I kinda do. I only said all that stuff about having to be angry in order to get him to put his guard down," Vernon replied.

"Don't be silly. We need him. He needs us. Whether either of you like this, we're in it together."

"And what about you? Don't you want to get revenge for your brother?" Vernon asked.

"Yes. But Lars didn't kill him. Hell, Lars had nothing to do with us being in The Hole in the first place, except indirectly. I think Rod set us up to find a way to kill my brother."

"Rod?" Lars asked, looking interested suddenly. "The hacker?"

"Why would he do that?" Vernon asked at the same time.

"Because James knew who he was. Who he really was," Elizabeth replied.

Lars laughed. "As a matter of fact, so do I," he said. "And I'm delighted to say that everything makes sense now. Also, he isn't a he. At least I don't think so."

"What?" Vernon and the princess asked together. It was nice to see she seemed as confused as he was.

"The hacker you're referring to isn't the maverick outsider you think he is. In fact, he's a persona the Faction created in the 1990s to gain acceptance in the hacker community, under a team of hackers who'd joined the cause. He's had a dozen names: Brown, Sked—that was actually the same guy before that particular operative went rogue on us—and now Rod. The ruse worked so well that we have some serious access through our network which any one individual lone-wolf hacker wouldn't be able to get. The computer intelligence unit took on a life of its own, and has since become our major source of financing. We rent it out to other organizations."

"Rod is one of you?" Elizabeth said. "I can't believe that. And I especially don't believe my brother would have gone along with any of this. I told you already: he knew who Rod really was."

"Did you ever meet Alyssa Rodanova?" Lars asked.

The princess's jaw dropped. "Yes. I always thought she and James were . . . I suppose 'lovers' is the right term, because she was married, if I recall correctly." Elizabeth paused. "We met her at a UN do in New York. She was on the board of one of the UNESCO children's charities we support. I was impressed. I thought that, for anyone barely thirty-five to have achieved so much in such a short time, she must have a very powerful personality."

"She does. She's also the main fundraiser for the Norwegian Faction. In fact, she is on our Steering Committee, with all that entails." Lars paused to look around. "She also leads the team that runs the Rod personality. In fact, she is the only person in the Faction who knows the names of the individuals currently on that team, as well as their location." He shrugged. "It never bugged me before, because compartmentalization is key for an organization like ours. But now, I'm terrified."

Elizabeth spoke grimly. "Not as terrified as she should be. Because I'm going to dedicate the rest of my life to killing her painfully."

Vernon knew he shouldn't speak, knew he would be best served sitting out the next few weeks in a deep hole somewhere, occasionally popping his head out of the sand to see who was winning the war that was about to start, but seeing Elizabeth's stern, beautiful features galvanized him. "And I'll help you every step of the way," he said.

By the time he regretted his words, it was too late to take them back.

Lars grinned and rubbed his hands. "It all makes sense now. Alyssa was always the one who argued for moderation in our methods. She was the only member of the Faction I ever knew that thought we should guide the development of BENT as opposed to eradicating them altogether. We all thought it was just because she was American and too nice for her own good."

"Rodanova?" Vernon asked. "That doesn't sound American."

"Her grandparents ran from the war. She grew up listening to stories about how everyone should be nicer to each other," Elizabeth said. "And she told them to us. Repeatedly. Hell, if it wasn't for the fact that she was utterly gorgeous, I never would have understood what James saw in her. Well, that and her money. And her almost hypnotic personality." She shook her head. "But other than that, a true mystery."

Vernon was delighted to see the spark of humor coming back to the princess, and even more, he hoped that his own willingness to help had allowed some of that warmth to return.

"She controls the best network of hackers and cybersecurity people in the world," Lars told them. "We're going to have a tough time going anywhere without popping up on their radars. They probably have access to more security cameras than anyone else. And that includes the Chinese government."

"That's why we're going to hit her before she knows we're coming. Before she has time to suspect we're even still alive, and before she can protect herself fully," Elizabeth said. "Did you tell her you were hiring this plane and the mercenaries?"

"No."

"Why not?"

"Because I was sure someone in the Faction was going to try to stage a coup. I was the senior operative on the field side of the Faction, and someone was playing head games with me, trying to get me to recommend pulling most everyone out of the field. I think the reason they wanted that was precisely so the attack on Antarctica would succeed while we were worried about the internal threats. That's why I dropped off the grid and headed there. I actually pretended that law enforcement was after me and initiated the go-to-ground protocol that all operatives have. After that, it was a question of moving fast."

"It's a good thing you did. Now we can surprise her," Elizabeth said.

"I'm sorry," Vernon interjected, "but how can we surprise Rod, or Rodanova, or whatever his name is? How the hell do you even know where he is? And why are we going to Mexico?"

Lars looked from Vernon to Elizabeth quizzically, one eyebrow raised.

The princess sighed. "I suppose explanations are in order."

"I think so," Lars replied. "And your compatriot appears to agree."

The princess held up the cylinder that Vernon had stolen from Jorgensen's deepest, most secret lab. It was plugged into a power socket using a USB cable.

"Rodanova knew what this was," she said.

"I believe we all do. It's property you took from Jorgensen Pharmaceutical."

Elizabeth shook her head. "This isn't property," she said. "This is a thinking, feeling entity. A true artificial intelligence, not the kind of plagiarism software kids use to cheat on assignment papers.

And Rodanova knew it. She had her people torturing it."

"How can you torture a computer?" Lars asked.

"They were depriving it of input, feeding back its own output into it so it could never get anything new, and then channeling noise through the system. Think of it as being in solitary confinement under arc lights and with loud, distorted music filling your cell twenty-four hours a day. That's what they were doing to this Brain." Now imagine someone opening the door to your cell and telling you that it was over, that it was all going to be all right. Well, to this Brain, I'm that someone. It's not going to let anyone hurt me, and it's been helping me track Rod."

"All well and good, but the system the hackers are using is mostly used to hide from exactly that kind of scrutiny," Lars said. "Rodanova's team has been doing it for years."

"Perhaps. But apparently, she has decided she needs to act quickly, and that meant being a little sloppy. And a Brain this size, even working at a tenth of its nominal capacity—because I can't cool it enough to make it work fully, or it will fry—can spot untidiness from orbit," Elizabeth said.

"So, why are we going to Mexico?"

"Because that's where Rod will be. Whether she is or isn't Rodanova."

"I have no doubt of it," Lars replied.

"And I'd love for it to be true," Elizabeth said. "Because I never really liked her. I guess we'll both find out when we get to Mexico."

"We'll never make it. As soon as the plane lands, half the Mexican army and the entire Mexico City police force will be on us. Benito Juarez airport is tight as a drum—the drug cartel wars have made certain of that: the government watches everything there."

"That's why we're not going anywhere near the airport."

"We have to land somewhere."

"We will. And it will be fine. In the meantime, I want to tell you a little bit about what's about to go down. Rod has decided that, in order to show the world that the balance of power has shifted and that no one needs to fear even the most powerful Talents anymore, he's going to kill the biggest, baddest BENT south of the Rio Grande."

"She's going after El Chapo," Lars said, shaking his head in admiration. "That's brilliant."

Vernon groaned. "And we have to save that scumbag's life? Unfair." He thought about it for a moment. "And besides, I always thought El Chapo was the dumbest superhero name ever invented."

Chapter 20

The pilot wasn't happy at all.

To be fair, the man hadn't been happy since the moment he'd learned he'd lost control of his aircraft to a computer rebellion of some sort. But compared to his current unhappiness, that had been nothing but mild irritation.

"We're all going to die," he said. "And we're probably going to kill a bunch of people doing it. Hell, we don't have enough fuel to make it back to Benito Juarez, so the humane thing to do would be to try to avoid the houses. There are still some patches of jungle over there. We should aim for those."

"Keep your course," Elizabeth said.

"Like I have a choice. Can't I go back there and tell the troops to say their final goodbyes?"

"No. I need you to land this thing. Manually, because . . . well, because it's going to be a little unorthodox."

"I already told you. There's no place to land. This is a city of twenty-odd million people. There are houses everywhere. And where there are no houses, there are trees. And the roads are packed. And they're too winding even if we could clear them. Trust me, I looked," the pilot replied.

Elizabeth stared out the window, then she pointed. "Can you land there? My computer tells me it's not programmed for uninstrumented landings, but I assume that if you managed Antarctica, you can do this."

"Son of a bitch," the pilot said. "Everyone out of my cabin and buckle in. We're only going to have one shot at this, because we're already running on fumes. Really. Get out, now."

Vernon, Lars, and Elizabeth piled into the lounge and buckled their belts. Wind buffeted the plane as they descended, and the pilot came on to the intercom. "This is your captain speaking. Hope everyone had a great flight. There's been a change of itinerary, and now, instead of refueling in the Azores, we'll be landing just outside Mexico City. I've been informed that we should be ready for combat as soon as we land, so please have your gear ready. Having said that, please wait for the airplane to come to a complete halt before descending. We're expecting a bumpy taxiway. But once it's done, you will be able to deplane immediately." There was a long pause. "Provided, of course, that we manage not to slam into any of the pyramids."

Vernon looked out the window to see a green landscape dotted with single-story houses. The dense urban sprawl he'd come to associate with Mexico's Federal District was nowhere to be seen. He didn't recognize the area.

Until he saw a long strip of open area, gray from the stone surface. It could, conceivably, have been a landing strip out in some wilderness had it not been for the pyramids lining it.

Teotihuacán was not something you forgot. Once you'd been to the site, you remembered it forever.

The plane was to land on the ancient city's central causeway, the narrow strip of exposed stone visible from the air. It banked for a moment, and the runway disappeared from Vernon's view. Seconds later, stone monuments began to flash past in the window, and the wheels connected with the ground. The plane slewed to one side, then the other, but it was losing speed. They were actually going to make it.

The smell of melting rubber filled the cabin, after a particularly deep rut in the stone path, and dust was suspended in the air.

Vernon grimaced. Even if they survived, this was going to be an expensive landing for whoever owned the plane.

He turned to Lars. "Hey, do you—"

He never finished. The plane slammed into something and somersaulted, the tail flying over the cabin. It landed upside down, and Vernon found himself suspended from his belt. Bits of glass, points blunted by the magic of his skin, adhered to his cheeks, and he wiped them away.

Then, holding on to the straps, he carefully undid the seatbelt buckles, hung for a moment, and then lowered himself onto the roof of the plane.

The lights had gone out, but there was plenty of light flooding through the plane's windows. He went to Elizabeth's seat. Blood dripped from her mouth, down to the roof. Vernon's heart beat quickly, but he felt a deadness inside. She wasn't moving at all.

Gently, he reached up to undo her buckle and let her drop into his arms. Then he lifted his eyes to look into her face, to search for any sign of life.

He found her staring back at him.

"I'm all right," she said. Her eyes were moist.

"Of course. I'll put you down."

She nodded, then leaned in and let her lips brush his, lightly enough that he wasn't sure she'd done it on purpose. He held her until she was standing firmly, then looked around the cabin.

Lars grimaced back at him. "Very touching. Now, do you think you can let me down so we can get this show on the road? I'm not going to be able to manage by myself."

Vernon approached and saw that Lars had a deep gash along his right arm that covered Vernon with blood as he worked the other man's belt. Lars helped as much as he could with his good hand, but it still took a certain amount of grunting and maneuvering before Lars was on the ground.

"Get the briefcase," Lars said. "I suspect we're going to need it."

"Why?" Elizabeth said. "Isn't this woman out to kill BENT? Why would she have them on her payroll?"

"Rodanova isn't the only person who is going to be out there. Do you fancy your chances with El Chapo? We just turned an important Mexican archaeological treasure into a plane crash site. He won't be happy. But maybe Vernon here can melt him."

Vernon sighed. "I'll get the suitcase."

They opened the door to the flight deck, but the pilot, copilot and stewardess had borne the brunt of the accident when the man-high stone platform that had halted their progress crushed the nose flat, and all three were extremely dead.

The troops in the main hold had fared better, but only in relative terms. In their case, the problem was that they'd ignored the injunctions to wear their seatbelts, and had been tossed around pretty badly by the crash. Only four of them were combat-ready, and a pair was unconscious and would need immediate medical attention.

"Damn it," Elizabeth said. "Don't mercenary companies believe in Master Sergeants? Had you had a good one of those, you wouldn't be sitting here like a bunch of little girls who scraped their knees. You four, look lively. Get your rifles and let's move." She turned toward the back of the plane. "I suppose the ramp is buggered. Help me with the door. Move!"

Vernon raised an eyebrow at her.

"What? Do you think princesses are exempt from military service? On the contrary, it's kind of obligatory. I did my stint in the Royal Marines. I wasn't even allowed to be with my brother for the hard stuff. So, I can curse with the best of them. Any problems with that?"

"No, ma'am," Vernon replied with a grin.

"Good."

The troops had gotten the door open.

Purple and orange light came through the opening.

"Looks like they started without us," Lars observed.

Chapter 21

The sky was a dark gray, bordering on black, except when multicolored lightning made it look like a swollen bruise. The bright blue of moments before the landing was gone, swallowed up by the war between powers.

The focus of all this fury was the pyramid at the end of the runway: Teotihuacán's Pyramid of the Sun, which towered above them, a monument to colossal engineering. The gray stone reflected the light from the raging skies and glowed angry purple and orange.

"Nice place for the end of the world," Vernon mused. "Quite atmospheric. I assume the guy up there, the little guy with the huge mustache, is El Chapo?"

"Unless someone else has the same bend, yeah," Lars replied. "Before all of this happened, I was looking forward to frying him with his own colored lightning. Never thought I'd be on a quest to save the fucker."

From what Vernon had read, El Chapo called himself the Successor of the Pantheon. He claimed to have inherited the combined powers of all the gods to have inhabited the territory of Mexico since the dawn of time. Mostly, however, he seemed to do tricks with the weather.

Lightning—regular white stuff, this time—slammed into the ground at the right of the pyramid, and the little group dove for cover under the bottom step of the structure.

"So, what do we do now?" Vernon asked.

Elizabeth pointed to the left. "Let's go around the other way," she said. "Maybe we can see what's happening without calling attention to ourselves. If we can get close enough, maybe the soldiers and I can shoot at Rodanova's people."

"Can't the Brain turn off the device?" Vernon asked.

"Not without access to a network," the princess replied. "And I doubt the ancient Aztecs installed wi-fi."

"What about cell phones?" Vernon replied. "I've got a couple of bars on mine."

"Maybe. Open up a hot spot."

While Vernon did that, they walked along the base of the pyramid, dubious cover that mainly kept them from seeing what any of the other belligerents were up to. Finally, they reached the far left corner of the colossal structure. Vernon poked his head around. "We'll have to keep walking. All I can see is a motor home that seems to have exploded. It's still sending up smoke."

"Why isn't Rodanova using the device on El Chapo?" Lars said.

"I can answer that," Elizabeth replied. "Or rather, the Brain can. The truck over there was supposed to beam the images worldwide, but El Chapo hit it with a bolt, so now Rodanova and her team are scrambling to get the broadcast running. She wants the whole world to see."

"How the hell does the Brain know that?" Lars said.

"Apparently, they're also using cell networks. Unfortunately, the device itself is on a separate channel with no connection to any network. Purely manual control."

"It figures," Vernon said. "Rod knows just how easy stuff is to hack. He'd keep everything offline. Or she. Or whoever."

They had just begun to walk cautiously along the back wall of the pyramid when the dark skies suddenly turned completely black and the world around them became murky. Fog seeped from the loam beneath their feet, wisping and curling into fantastic shapes.

Though there had been no rain, a hailstorm clattered onto the pyramid . . . but not one stone fell directly on the ground. The group was pelted with ricochets, but every fragment of ice hit the building first.

"I think Rodanova is using the device," Lars said.

"You're right," Elizabeth said. "The Brain says there's a live transmission going on, showing what's happening here. You can probably see it on your phone. Not yours, Vern. We need the bandwidth for the Brain."

"Umm . . . then you definitely need to know that I'm running at 2 percent battery life."

"What? Why didn't you charge your phone?"

Vernon shrugged. "We were going to Antarctica. I assumed cell towers would be kinda few and far between, and that cafés with free wi-fi weren't going to be on the corner of ice road and snow street."

"Mine's smashed," Lars said.

"In that case, it looks like we'll have to do this the hard way," Elizabeth said.

"I could have sworn that was already what we were doing."

"No. What we were doing was to try to get in range to have the Brain take down Rodanova's electronics. That's not going to happen now."

Rain lashed at them, stinging, freezing, nearly horizontal, driven by a wind that appeared to circle the pyramid, as if Dorothy's cyclone had relocated itself from Kansas to try to uproot the massive stone edifice.

"She's working up to the big finale," Lars said. "We'd better hurry."

"The Brain just lost coverage. Your battery must have died, Vern," Elizabeth said.

Pushed by the wind at their back, they ran toward the edge of the pyramid to see a blonde woman in a black leather jumpsuit speaking into a camera, while several other cameras were trained on the top of the pyramid.

"That's her!" Lars shouted. "Fire!"

The four soldiers dropped to their knees and began shooting. Vernon saw one camera operator spin around, his camera flying as if he'd thrown it, before falling to his knees. Another simply crumpled where she stood.

Rodanova must have seen them coming. She dove behind a pile of equipment, and Vernon lost sight of her.

Elizabeth took aim and fired as well. A silver box arrayed in front of the pile sparked.

"You missed," Vernon said.

Elizabeth looked up. "Are you sure?" As if on cue, the skies cleared, and the rain stopped.

A monumental roar echoed between the jungle-covered hills that surrounded the site.

"That's El Chapo. And he sounds pissed."

Thunder rolled.

Preceded by the soldiers, Vernon, Elizabeth, and Lars ran to the small clearing vacated by Rodanova's film crew.

Lars bent over the box Elizabeth had shot, popped a clasp, and looked inside. He nodded to her. "Good thinking," he said.

Vernon nudged it with the toe of his foot. "Is this the device?"

"No. It's an amplifier. Without this, the device in Rodanova's possession is only good for a hundred feet or so." He glanced up to the top of the pyramid. "Not quite enough to reach that big meanie over there."

Lightning came out of the clear sky. A tree nearby exploded, and one of Lars's soldiers was set alight. He screamed and ran into a patch of dense vegetation, leaving behind the scent of charred flesh.

"Down!" Elizabeth screamed.

They ran back the way they'd come, to a point on the corner of the pyramid's base, where a jumble of stones created an overhang—a place where lightning couldn't reach them.

"We need to stop that nutjob!" Vernon screamed.

"This should help," Lars said. He handed Elizabeth a cell phone. "It belongs to that dead woman over there. She was filming with it when we shot her, and the screen hasn't locked down yet. We can use it."

"Set up a hotspot," Elizabeth said.

"Done," Lars replied. "I changed the password to 'hello.'"

"Okay. The Brain is in. How close do we need to be for that suitcase of yours to work?"

"This is a long-range version of the device. We're good from here," Lars replied.

The wind stopped. The air went still.

"The Brain has control of El Chapo's bend. Now, let's go find that Rodanova bitch," Elizabeth said.

They rushed into the trees. The clump was densely packed—it became obvious that the site's maintenance people dedicated themselves to the pyramids and ignored the foliage off the main paths—and they lost time pushing through.

"Where is everyone?" Vernon asked.

"Huh?" Lars said.

"We flew all night. It was morning when we crashed, and it might be dark because of all the weather problems, but I assume it's about ten o'clock, right? So, where the hell are the tourists? Last time I was here, you could barely move for all the people, even though this site is the size of Manhattan or something."

"Good question," Elizabeth said. She subvocalized something. A moment later, she spoke again. "The Brain says they authorities were aware that something big was about to go down, and they closed off all access."

"Which means the Mexican army is waiting to see who walks out of here alive and then arresting them? Comforting."

They came to a small clearing in the foliage where a single overweight man was bent over a large console under an awning. He appeared completely oblivious to their approach until one of the soldiers put the muzzle of his rifle against his cheek. Then he looked up, and his eyes widened.

The man took out a pair of earphones and Vernon winced. The music was loud all the way over here.

"Where is she?" Elizabeth asked, placing her own rifle against the man's sweaty forehead. The ice princess, the cold, calculating voice of command, was back.

Vernon reflected that, had he been on the wrong side of that gun, he would have known, deep in his bones, that the woman addressing him would have no problem in pulling the trigger.

The man pointed to a well-beaten path that emerged from the clearing in almost the exact same direction the team had come in from. "Th . . . That way."

Elizabeth nodded to the soldier who'd reached the guy first, and he slammed the butt of his AK into the back of the fat guy's neck. The console-jockey must have been tougher than he looked, because it took a second whack to put him under.

"We need to move," Lars said. "If they get close enough to use their device, they can kill El Chapo and disappear."

They raced out of the clearing in the direction the guy at the console had indicated.

Vernon thought. "What if we release El Chapo?" he asked. "Let them beat each other to pieces, and we can immobilize his bend again when we get closer."

Lars and Elizabeth exchanged glances, making Vernon feel like he was the junior member of the team, which was probably accurate. "He's right," Lars said, which did little to make Vernon feel better. Elizabeth's curt nod only made it worse.

The wind immediately picked up again. Freezing rain sprinkled the ground, and a violent gust of wind nearly swept Vernon off his feet.

"Someone is having a tantrum," Lars said.

"Wouldn't you?" Elizabeth asked. "I absolutely would. If I had my powers back, I'd level this entire site, just out of frustration for not being able to use them for ten days. And I have much better impulse control than El Chapo."

Vernon pointed to the top of the pyramid, visible above the trees. "I think El Chapo might be thinking along the same lines."

A human form—tiny from down at the base where the group had arrived—floated above the pyramid in a nimbus of light. *"Muerte!"* a voice like thunder roared.

Lightning of all colors shot from the black clouds onto the pyramid, the ground around it and the countryside in the distance. A cyclone lifted soil and rocks and hurled them through the air in every direction. There was no control this time, no containment. This was pure destruction at its worst.

Vernon stood beside Elizabeth, trying to shield her from any physical attack, and wondering whether his skin would defend him against electricity. Could it create some kind of conductor around him to deflect the charge? Or would he simply fry like the rest?

At least, no matter what happened, he would never know. If he was struck, he would be dead, or he would be alive, and in the latter case, he'd only become aware of it after the fact.

"What is he doing?" Elizabeth asked, looking up the pyramid. "It would only take one well-aimed bolt to fry Rodanova."

"I don't think he's fully in control of his powers," Lars replied. "I think Rodanova's device is right at the edge of its range . . . which means that it's probably interfering with his control."

"She's still climbing though, look." Vernon pointed to a small group ascending the pyramid well ahead of them.

A concentrated barrage of lightning slammed into the tip of the pyramid. Light blinded Vernon, but not before he saw enormous chunks of stone fly into the air.

"Down!" he shouted, and pushed Lars and Elizabeth into a heap below him, trying to cover them with his body.

A chunk of rock the size of a sofa landed on top of Vernon. He felt only a slight pressure as his chemical factory somehow dissolved the rock as it came into contact with him, before it could transfer its momentum into his body. The rock actually broke into rubble from the impact.

Of course, all of the clothes on his back dissolved as it happened.

He stood, the front of his wardrobe hanging like a limp flag, and pulled Elizabeth to her feet.

When he held out a hand to Lars, the other man shook his head in wonder. "You saved me. Her, I can understand, but me . . . I don't know if I'd have done the same for you."

"You're a complete dickhead," Vernon said. "But right now, you're on my team."

The soldiers had survived, although one of them suffered a nasty gash on the forehead. They'd sensed the danger and had pressed themselves against one of the stepped ridges of the pyramid.

The man with the gash looked pale. He was bleeding profusely. "I think I'm going to have to stop here," he said.

"You, bandage his head and come after us when you're done," Lars said to another of the troops.

They resumed their tortuous climb up the slope.

"We should have gone up the front," Vernon said. "There are stairs on that one."

"Yeah. It was also the way he was looking at the time, which meant he would have spotted us immediately," Elizabeth reminded them. "Not the healthiest option."

"Maybe we should just let Rodanova kill the sucker," Vernon said. "Then we kill her and get the hell out of here."

"No," Elizabeth replied. "No more BENTS get killed just for being BENT."

"How about for playing too many lightning tricks?"

The lightning hadn't killed El Chapo. He was still floating in his nimbus of light like some martyred saint in a renaissance fresco.

It had also failed to kill Rodanova, who, with only a single member of her retinue remaining, was climbing the side of the pyramid grimly, still up ahead.

"I think she's in range now," Lars said.

The evidence appeared to support his claim, as the weather had begun to behave a little more normally. As Vernon watched, El Chapo's light show flickered and went out, and he dropped heavily to the rubble on the apex of the pyramid.

"He won't last long," Lars said.

"Can you try to balance out whatever she's doing?" Elizabeth asked.

"It's very risky. If we happen to reinforce one of her commands . . ."

"Yeah, he could die," Elizabeth said. "But he definitely will die if we don't do anything."

"I wasn't thinking about El Chapo," Lars said. "This guy is a serious Talent. If we reinforce a weather-attack command, we could create a serious event. We could all die."

"We still need to try," Elizabeth replied.

Lars fiddled with the cell phone, and Vernon hoped no one decided to point one of those devices at him. He didn't know how it chose the victim, but he'd felt what his own power could do to him under commands from that machine, and wanted no part of experiencing that ever again.

In the meantime, he'd outdistanced the preoccupied Lars and the tiring Elizabeth by two levels. He would reach the showdown, if there was a showdown, well ahead of his team. Well, someone had to do it, and the remaining soldier seemed to feel that his duty was to guard Lars . . . and not be the first to arrive at the spot where the shit was expected to hit the fan.

He'd closed the gap on Rodanova and her lackey, but they would arrive at the top before he did. He pulled himself up another block. Another. He tried to hurry, but he wasn't going to make it.

Vernon was still two blocks down when the two women ahead reached the summit.

He didn't care if El Chapo died today. By all accounts, the man was a dangerous megalomaniac who deserved anything that happened to him, but Vernon knew that Elizabeth had her heart set on the Mexican Talent surviving the confrontation, and he wanted to give her that piece of solace in what was a dark time for her.

"Kill him," a woman's voice drifted down to him. As he crested the final block, he saw the voice was Rodanova's. The blonde woman was leaning over a short-haired, chubby woman who must have been the technician assigned to the device. The apparatus itself was a gray oblong of metal with screens and dials covering one surface.

"I'm trying," the tech replied. "There's something wrong with the box."

Rodanova grunted. "Then we'll do this the old-fashioned way," she said. "No one said this fucker was bulletproof."

She pulled a pistol from her belt and pointed it at the middle of El Chapo's head.

Vernon arrived to push the muzzle away just as she pulled the trigger.

The gun melted under his touch, and he turned to face the immediate danger: the technician at the device.

That woman looked at him long and hard and began to play with dials. Vernon rushed her, intending to take her hands off the machine but, just before he reached her, he felt his skin begin to tingle and panicked.

Instead of removing the tech's hand, he kicked her in the face. The force of the kick jerked her to her feet and over the side of the pyramid with enough energy that she flew past the first ledge, barely clipped the second and then bounced off the edge of each successive step just hard enough to flip herself out again to hit the next edge, like a person falling all the way down a set of gigantic stairs. After the second impact, her scream ceased.

Rodanova's own scream tore Vernon's attention away from the crumpled form that eventually landed on one ledge. He saw El Chapo advancing on the woman he'd known as Rod, hands outstretched and lightning playing between his fingers. Evidently, when the bad guys had redirected their own machine toward Vernon, El Chapo had come free.

He wondered whether the right course of action would be to just let El Chapo torture her to death. She definitely deserved it.

But he'd already killed a woman he had no intention of killing. He knew that saving her boss would make zero difference to the dead tech down there who was just trying to do her job, but the idea of saving Rodanova galvanized him. He stepped between the helpless woman and the approaching Mexican nightmare.

El Chapo blinked and focused on Vernon. "*Estupidísimo,*" he muttered.

Vernon found himself engulfed in light. He could almost feel the heat of the lightning strike.

But when the world went dark again, he found himself still intact, albeit almost blinded.

All he could see was El Chapo's face, completely shocked to find something other than ashes in his path.

Vernon put his entire weight behind a single massive right hook that landed right on the point of the Mexican's chin.

El Chapo went down like the proverbial poleaxed steer.

Vernon fell right beside him. His skin suddenly burned so badly that he couldn't keep himself on his feet. He tried to move his mouth, to scream to someone to turn off the device, but moving his mouth hurt too much.

He'd fallen with his face toward the device. With infinite care, he focused his eyes.

Rod. Or Rodanova. Or whoever the fuck the sicko who wanted the device to further their own agenda might be, was glaring at him and turning the control knob.

Vernon wanted to scream, but instead saw a flicker of movement and smiled. The expression tore at his burning flesh, and he wanted to scream again.

But only for a few more seconds. The seconds it took for Elizabeth to finish climbing over the ledge, pull the blonde woman to her feet, rush her to the side of the pyramid and send her, screaming, over the edge to join her tech before turning the pain back down to zero.

He blacked out in relief.

Chapter 22

"How does this feel?" Elizabeth asked, running a fingernail softly over the skin of his back.

"Wonderful," Vernon replied. "It's so intense. Makes me feel more alive than I have in ages."

His skin had grown back, brand new and more sensitive than ever, and within days, Vernon had been back on his feet. Elizabeth had nursed him back to health and now sat beside him on a beach café in a resort town just south of the city of Ouidah in Benin.

They'd asked if they could be served on the beach, and the proprietor had smiled and dragged a table and two chairs out onto the sand.

"How about this?" Elizabeth asked, and kissed the nape of his neck.

Vernon sighed and turned his head to catch her lips with his own. Being in close proximity to her in a small room open to the sea breezes had led from one thing to another.

And it had led to multiple, vigorous anothers.

The kiss ended, and he gazed over the slightly brownish—kind of orange—sand, sand mixed with the red inland soil, into the depths of the South Atlantic.

"*Centime* for your thoughts," Elizabeth said.

She was the one who'd chosen the destination. She was the one who spoke decent French. And she was the one who told him that no one would ever think to look in Benin, of all places, for the two people the world held responsible for the near-destruction—along with El Chapo, who'd been unceremoniously tossed in The Hole—of the cultural treasure of Teotihuacán. She was also the one who'd somehow gotten him out of Mexico before the authorities could grab his unconscious form and drop him in the next cell.

Well, he assumed the Brain was helping to cover their tracks as well.

Elizabeth told him that the reason she chose Benin was that the Ouidah Voodoo festival was coming, and that it was worth staying around for. And she hadn't asked a single uncomfortable question during the whole process.

Until now.

"Do you miss Maia?" she asked. "You can talk to me. I know what it's like to have someone I love die on me."

Vernon stared at her. "Am I really that easy to read?" he asked.

"It's not difficult to read a man staring out to sea in that way. Not difficult at all."

He laughed, long and hard, feeling happy for the first time in years. "Well, Miss Princess Smartypants, you're wrong on every count except that, yeah, I miss her a bit. But I was never in love with her. I knew it, and she knew it. We were just holding each other up until one or the other could find a better support."

"Is that what I am?" Elizabeth asked. "A better support?"

He shook his head. "I don't think so . . . I . . ." Vernon's voice trailed off. "This is hard for me. Last time . . ."

"I know," she said.

"So, you understand that this isn't about Maia. It's about whether I'm ready for this." His gesture encompassed the beach, the sea, Elizabeth, and the entire world. He didn't exactly know what it included, but they both knew what he meant.

"So, what are you going to do about that?" she asked.

"Nothing. I'm not going to wreck this just because I'm psychologically broken. I'm going to give it a chance."

"Wow. I wasn't expecting that," Elizabeth said. "In my experience, people are more complicated than that. More twisted."

"I've done twisted for four years. I didn't like it much. I want to give normal a chance again."

She leaned over and kissed him. "That's a bit of a relief," she said. "I would have hated to have to compete with Maia's ghost. I kind of liked her, and it's impossible to beat a ghost."

"Oh, that was never a problem," Vernon replied. "Maia isn't dead."

"She got teleported into outer space, Vernon."

"Yeah. And unless that machine's range was a lot wider than Lars told us, she teleported straight back to Earth as soon as she arrived to find herself out of device range. Why would a teleport stay in space and suffocate? He should have used the thing to teleport different parts of her body to different places. That would have killed her. But not this."

He laughed at her expression.

Elizabeth leaned over and kissed him.

We hope that you enjoyed this title and look forward to many more to come. Please, leave us a review! Reviews matter to all of our authors.

And don't forget to check out the latest edition of **Car Wars**

http://www.sjgames.com/car-wars/

Or the other amazing titles from
Steve Jackson Games

http://www.sjgames.com

…or the latest in the Car Warriors: Autoduel Chronicle fiction series. https://threeravenspublishing.com/car-warriors-autoduel-chronicles/

Take a look at some of our other award-winning series at
https://threeravenspublishing.com/series-universes/

Visit us at
https://www.threeravenspublishing.com and sign up for our newsletter for the latest and greatest news on upcoming titles and events.

Other series and titles you might enjoy.

B.E.N.T.
BIOLOGIC   ENHANCED   NASCENT   TALENT
ANNOYED
WITH
LLOYD
CHRISTOPHER WOODS

DECLAN FINN
DECLAN FINN
DECLAN FINN DECLAN FINN
Demons Are Forever
Honor At Stake
Live And Let Bite
Good To The Last Drop
The Dragon Award Nominated Series
FREE on Kindle Unlimited!

AVAILABLE ON
AMAZON
JOINT TASK FORCE
13
HOLDING THE LINE
BETWEEN HEAVEN AND HELL
13

MYSTERY,
MAGIC &
MAYHEM
WITH A TWIST
OF ROMANCE
J.F. POSTHUMUS
ON AMAZON
FIND ME

Gustavo Bondoni

STARFLIGHT

You can also keep up to date with our latest release announcements on <u>Scifi.radio</u> and get some of the best fandom programing on the planet.

Scifi for your Wifi

And don't forget to check out our other Sponsors and Affiliates

A southern Appalachian jewel for craft beer lovers, Buck Bald Brewing offers something for everyone. With delicious, locally brewed beverages from across the spectrum, Buck Bald Brewing offers craft brews that are consistently amazing.

From the dark and smooth Shesquatch Scottish ale, to the intense hops of

Hippibilly IPA, to the puckering sour of the blackberry and cinnamon in Berry My Heart at the Trailer Park, and more than 60+ rotating brews, you'll find what you're looking for and more.

With smiling faces behind the bar ready to help you find your next favorite brew, a constantly rotating selection of delicious craft beverages, toe-tapping tunes always playing, and the biggest games on TV, you can kick your feet up in either Copperhill, Tennessee or Murphy, North Carolina and immerse yourself in the Buck Bald Brewing experience. So, come out, fill a pint, fill a growler, and fill your mind at your new favorite family-owned craft brewery.

To discover more visit us at buckbaldbrewing.com or follow us on Facebook @buckbaldbrewing and @buckbaldbrewingmurphy.

Vesper Wren's
TRAILER PARK
PIXIE
PUNCH
· A PEACH STRAWBERRY SELTZER ·
BUCK BALD BREWING

BRAXTON
HICKS
MIDNIGHT MOCHA MILK
STOUT
BUCK BALD BREWING

www.ingramcontent.com/pod-product-compliance
Lightning Source LLC
Chambersburg PA
CBHW020059310726
48970CB00002B/396